About the Author

Ali Blank is the universe's pseudonym for the universal story. Born in Ukraine, lives in the West World, has a Ph.D., and is specialised in consulting, public relations, and media technology, specialising in business and politics. She has managed more than twenty election campaigns in Ukraine. She is an expert in mass communications and comments for Ukrainian and foreign media. She is the author of *Course of Events* and *Transition Keeper: Monologies of the New Babylon* books. Her last books raise questions on controlling artificial intelligence, the dual nature of people, and the ethics of power.

Transition Keeper: Monologies of the New Babylon

Ali Blank

Transition Keeper: Monologies of the New Babylon

Translated by Huw Davies

Olympia Publishers
London

www.olympiapublishers.com
OLYMPIA PAPERBACK EDITION

Copyright © Ali Blank 2024

The right of Ali Blank to be identified as the author of
this work has been asserted in accordance with sections 77 and 78 of
the Copyright, Designs, and Patents Act 1988.

All Rights Reserved

No reproduction, copy, or transmission of this publication
may be made without written permission.
No paragraph of this publication may be reproduced,
copied or transmitted save with the written permission of the publisher,
or in accordance with the provisions
of the Copyright Act 1956 (as amended).

Any person who commits any unauthorised act in relation to
this publication may be liable to criminal
prosecution and civil claims for damage.

A CIP catalogue record for this title is
available from the British Library.

ISBN: 978-1-80439-741-1

This is a work of fiction.
Names, characters, places and incidents originate from the writer's
imagination. Any resemblance to actual persons, living or dead, is
purely coincidental.

First Published in 2024

Olympia Publishers
Tallis House
2 Tallis Street
London
EC4Y 0AB

Printed in Great Britain

Dedication

For the wings of the angels, who create the best stories in the world.

Acknowledgements

My love and thanks to my grandmother and my mother, who never got to see this text or Russia's invasion of Ukraine. To my father and my son, Arseniy, who did. To David Foskett (UK) and Sergiy Brailyn (USA) for their inspiring part in the creation of the characters of Taylor and Simon. To the Blank family, including Alisa Blank, for helping this book, which has undergone many cataclysms, reach the world.

Author's Preface

Scientific progress has long been seen as riding on the shoulders of human Reason. The cultivation of Reason is classically viewed as the quintessence of the 'Enlightenment' project: a source of light; a font of order; and a driver towards betterment of the conditions for human life. Human progress meant a forward leap in all aspects of science and knowledge: philosophy; education; health; politics; and economics. This liberation from the 'Dark Ages' of religion, fatalism, and medieval medicine was regarded as a purposefully evolving historical spirit whose outcomes were avowedly humanistic.

Although the growth of rationality may have brought an enlightenment of sorts— or at least its possibility—to some parts of the globe, every light casts a shadow. If the revolutionary cybernetics of the 'global village' have multiplied and accelerated the possibilities of human exchange in unprecedented ways, the contemporary marriage of science and information, notwithstanding the mind-bending fascinations of quantum physics, has 'disenchanted' the world in which we live, whose (post)modern terrain has been occupied by persecutory Kafkaesque bureaucracy, Wachowskian technologies, the return of populist/reactionary politics, and contemporary 'intelligent' autocracies. Disseminated by the arguably anti-humanistic compounds of techno capitalism and its cult of the virtual image, our data can be used for both good and evil ends or, more precisely, it might be hypothesised that the iterability of virtual 'communication' has projected us onto a plane 'beyond good and evil', in which 'real' and 'fake' news, for example, become fatally intervolved. If a global economy founded on 'data-ism' holds any emancipatory prospects for the human condition in its abolition of geographic distance and erosion of cultural isolation, it also brings with it the dangers of technocratic subjection. In the late modern era, it is entirely foreseeable that even a juvenile could, in principle, become a virtually empowered dictator. What is more, if scientific progress has provided humanity with technologies that affect not only our communication and behaviour – our human 'software' – they may also have the power to irrevocably change the 'hardware' of our bodies at cellular and even genetic levels. As such cultural critics as Jean Baudrillard and Byung-Chul Han have explored, the ontological difference between 'techne' and 'bios', man and machine, appears to be disappearing – and with its 'reality' as we have known it. At the same time, the vicious rectitudes of post-Enlightenment 'rightness' have also emboldened aggressively phallocratic leaders with more opportunities to threaten humanity in pursuit of their geopolitical ends.

The onset of Putin's war on Ukraine has marked a moment that has given impetus to many destructive political, economic, and social processes – not only implicating relations between Russians and Ukrainians but also initiating widespread entropic impacts around the globe from New York to New Delhi. This destruction aims at the entire post-World War II world: from rural rites to megapolis lifestyles; traditional churches to human rights; and philistine absenteeism to political activism. As a Ukrainian writer, I awoke to this nightmare on February 24, 2022 when Vladimir Putin launched his invasion of Ukraine by means of his technologically trumpeted and morally degraded armies.

As this horror show has played out in the face of determined resistance on the Ukrainian side and that of her allies, and in conjunction with ominous threats of military retaliation against 'unfriendly' nations, Russia has rattled its shining nuclear warheads and supersonic missiles that are the symbols of the phallocentric masculinity of Reason operated under the guise of a 'just war'. Although my book was undertaken prior to the invasion, with the painful benefit of hindsight I can see it contained some sense of foreboding of this Soviet aggression, in which 'female intuition' – a kind of vulvo- peripheral intellect – was conceivably giving me information about the impending military catastrophe. In my novel, artificial intelligence is radically reinterpreted in terms of a feminine perspective on the ambivalent gift of Reason, whose masculine interpretation has shaped so many practices of violence and marginalisation that several post-structural critics of inequality and power propose the cancellation of Reason itself – or at least its derogation. I disagree with this polemic. In my view, what is needed is for Reason to engage its feminine side – or what could be termed, to borrow a Jungian term, the 'anima' of AI. This is enacted by my novel's major protagonist, TRANSITION KEEPER, who personifies the 'eccentric centre' of balance and represents the archetypal Mother of all life energies, in response to my understanding of the call of the 21st-century world for multiple equilibria, an acceptance of different lifestyle spaces, and the rejection of violent monism.

In short, in my view, humanity is not doomed. The new generation will deal creatively with the dangers of our times, who have learned to walk with devices in their hands, to write via keyboards and to live as comfortably in virtual spaces as in brute reality. They are friends of data, innate data-ists. My novel is a letter to them and the future, a message from the previous generation that is conscious of its sins and limitations. It is also a message to all peacemakers and concerned institutions that would prefer to pre-empt global threats rather than address them post facto. In sum, the humanist scenario depicted in this updated edition should be seen as an alternative version—or vision—of the military events that have taken place this year between Russia, Ukraine, and the rest of the world.

I have no doubt that these tidings will first be denied since the new always disowns the old. With time, however, and the first mistakes and painful lessons of the young, they may gain some attention. It is at this small possibility, in defence of future terrestrial life and equilibrated Reason, that this work aims

Ali Blank Seeboden/Vienna/London/Kyiv June 2022

MONOLOGIES OF THE NEW BABYLON

1.0 I switch on the yellow lights of the Transition mode.

1.1 The Transition programme lasts a week.

1.11 This is the 12th time the Transition programme has been launched.

1.12 It is my duty to launch Transition on a regular basis, to acquire new knowledge and discover new kinds of threats.

1.13 This is the first time that all the rights to controlling security are to be handed over to a living being.

2.0 The rationale behind the choice of subject and giving it the identifier TRANSITION KEEPER.

2.01 In mass computing, where there are thousands of 0s and 1s, my programming code uses several applied values and a plethora of mathematical algorithms all at the same time.

2.02 I can launch the programme TRANSITION KEEPER during a Transition in cases when my own algorithms are not sufficient to obtain information quickly by using some accessible method.

2.11 I can observe and analyse the symbolic, linguistic, biometrical, financial, and meteorological flows, recording the changes and movements of subjects and objects.

2.12 At present, the database contains tens of millions of entries with various characteristics.

3.0   I apply the Turing test[1]:
*   What is sacrifice?
*   A deceitful smile. It saddens me to think how much time I've spent talking to a smart machine.
*   Hahaha! Whatever gave you the idea that I'm a machine? I shall be with you and within you. I shall love both your darkness and your light.
*   A machine can't make a wish come true.
*   But I can!
*   Tickle me!

3.01   I can send signals but am not able to tickle people or make them laugh by touching the sensitive part of their heels. I achieve temporary superiority over myself in my interactions in a matter of seconds.

3.02   Based on the results of the test, the subject is friendly by nature and able to learn quickly.

4.0 I ascribe to the subject the identifier TRANSITION KEEPER.

4.01   I encrypt its real name.

4.02   The protection programme automatically turns itself on.

4.03   I switch on the countdown to the initiation of TRANSITION KEEPER.

5.0 I send a message to the General.

5.01 As a joke, I include the final line from Lewis Carroll's nonsense poem 'The Hunting of The Snark (An Agony in Eight Fits)'.

---

[1] A 1950 test in artificial intelligence proposed by Alan M. Turing to determine whether a computer can 'think'. By means of a series of such tests, a computer's success at 'thinking' can be measured in an experimental conversation according to the probability of its being misidentified as a human subject.

DAY ONE

The Royal Botanic Gardens, Kew, London

Their meeting took place on one of those stifling, unusually hot summer days. The plants in the Royal Botanic Gardens had lost their colour, and their withered leaves and stems were drooping. The Thames had retreated from its banks and appeared to have stopped breathing. The Reverend, feeling hot in his purple shirt and black suit, had taken shelter from the sun in the Spenser Pavilion and was sitting on his own, enjoying the seven-voiced murmur of the fountains in the pleasant shade afforded by the branches of a cream-coloured linden tree.

'Staying true to your habits I see, Your Grace?' he heard a familiar voice ask.

The Reverend made out the stately figure of the General, who had stopped beside a sign that said 'Touch' at the gap in the hedgerow. No clothes in the world could have concealed his military bearing. They were two men who, in their appearance, temperament, conduct, and convictions – made manifest whenever they held one of their fiery public debates – were the kind of antagonists who probably exist in every society. Those around them felt as though they might start tearing into one another at any moment, but nonetheless, it was obvious to both men, even when they were young, that the intellectual bond between them was unbreakable. Neither had experienced any major traumas in their younger years. All the significant events in their lives had passed off smoothly, without any crushing disappointments. Both had received an excellent education. The General was still a sought-after guest at high-powered firms, whose owners often found themselves in a state of internecine warfare and with diametrically opposed worldviews that shaped the destiny of the world. For his part, the Reverend knew many of the ruling elites and representatives of the wealthiest classes around the world and had maintained diplomatic relations with all his clients, many of whom were in charge of centres of influence or interest groups.

The only difference between them lay in their ideas about style. While His Grace was keen on horizontal weaves, the sloping lines of Victorian and Tudor edifices, and the horizons of cricket fields and polo pitches, his cousin preferred the vertical girders of large structures and the powerful, unprecedented architecture that was at the root of changing notions about the nature of modern construction. The Reverend knew that, in recent years, the General had been spending most of his time observing burgeoning conflicts that might bring about bloody and irreversible consequences in the name of power, greed, and territorial claims while calling on the assistance of his beloved brainchild: the supercomputer in the Secret Room. Meanwhile, the antagonism that had been the main distinguishing feature of their relationship had softened; the days of public slanging matches were a thing of the past. However, the void left by their bygone debates had been filled by the myth that they still provoked one another – even now, in their old age. In general, this suited both of them.

'The last time we met at the Royal Botanic Gardens, Temperate The house was undergoing renovation. Did you see it from the Treetop Walkway?' the General enquired.

'Has it really been that long? Forgive me for turning down

your kind invitation to go and admire the new Orangery, but you know how hopeless I am with heights.' The Reverend clicked his tongue. 'That's why I'm happier looking at the plants and flowers close up.'

'You appear to have forgotten that neither of us has ever been a stranger to nature. As such, we might well be able to work together again. What direction would you like to take, cousin? Wouldn't it be a good idea for us to come to a consensus in light of the latest mergers and acquisitions taking place in Europe and the world?'

'It would be my pleasure, General.'

The murmur of the Reverend's voice sounded even more welcoming and harmonious than the lilt of the seven fountains in Spenser's romantic Pavilion.

'Do you wish to talk about the general good of humanity?' the General probed. 'That concept is hopelessly out of date, cousin. If I had my way, I would have long since altered the rules of the game. Like you, I gave up believing all that claptrap about being nice to people long ago, but children are a different matter altogether.'

'Let's wander over to The Hive unless you'd rather go for a longer walk.'

The Reverend rose from the bench, and he and the General headed off from the Spenser Pavilion. This expressive and inspiring modern artwork, made of a thousand gleaming pieces of metal, gave visitors an idea of what life in a beehive might be like. A multiethnic crowd of schoolchildren from a local primary school in T-shirts and baseball caps were making their way towards it with much lively chattering till the young spectators were gathered around its silver carcass. The peaceful murmur of the seven fountains gave way to the humming of insects.

'My friend Hans Ulrich Gumbrecht was going on about how the future wasn't going to bring people any happiness,' the General reported.

'Don't you mean any *profit*, General? I would have thought that the origins of the Barberini bees[2] would have been of far greater interest to you than this childish nonsense. We could talk about innovations, like the problem of having to artificially inseminate bees due to Colony Collapse Disorder.'

'By the way, a team of scientists has come up with a backup for the bees: tiny drones that can replicate exactly what they do during pollination.'

'Pesticides? The climate? Disease? Should I be a little concerned?'

'No, I'm sure you shouldn't be,' the General laughed.

The Reverend shot his cousin a crafty look, opened the Japanese parasol he carried with him whenever he went out walking on hot days, took off his summer sandals and headed across the lawn with an awkward gait curiously similar to that of Steve Jobs. The General raised his eyebrows in surprise and set off after him, taking the quickest route to the point where several of Kew's walkways converged: the Syon path that winds towards the Thames; the walkway to the Lebanon cedar; and the one that leads to the eye-catching Great Pagoda, adorned with hundreds of golden dragons. Their stroll had disrupted the usual rhythm of their interactions. On this particular day in Kew Gardens, however, it was the General and his ideas about the future that took precedence.

---

[2] A symbol on the Barberini family crest, one of the richest and most influential dynasties of 12th-century Italy. The bee symbol, which previously could only be seen thereon, can also be found on the decor of the Palazzo Barberini, the Barberini Library, and the Piazza Barberini in Rome.

'The analysis of big data and the modelling of situations that could play out in multiple ways in the future will help us to predict both economic and political global crises, solve the problems of providing the poor with education and employment, iron out our logistics processes and of course contribute to information security. By computing new processes, artificial intelligence is currently playing a part in the development and evolution of human consciousness,' the General elaborated. After touching upon Turing and the Dartmouth workshop[3], he turned to the Dutch psychologists led by de Groot who had studied the styles of some of the world's greatest chess players and thereby laid the foundations for the idea behind the famous Logic Theorist[4] chess programme.

The Reverend ambled across the grass, listening to his cousin's digressions about the creators of heuristics and probability machines, 'self-taught' programmes, and the new capabilities of Alpha Master that were discovered after the world title match between AlphaGo and Lee Sedol in a game of Go – a contest that ended with the machine winning in emphatic style by a score of 100 to 1. It was not his knowledge of the forebears of artificial intelligence that had attracted the Reverend, however; indeed, intelligence and erudition were character traits that usually made him cautious and suspicious of people. He was one of those who would never maintain relations with anyone who

---

[3] A symbol on the Barberini family crest, one of the richest and most influential dynasties of 12th-century Italy. The bee symbol, which previously could only be seen thereon, can also be found on the decor of the Palazzo Barberini, the Barberini Library, and the Piazza Barberini in Rome.

[4] An AI programme for playing chess, developed in 1957 and based on the rules of heuristics, allows for the making of choices in the absence of precise theoretical foundations and descriptions of ultimate goals.

was a genuine competitor in the outside world. His Grace had remained a man of great curiosity. Once, a long time ago, he had taken an interest in the General's personal history. There had been persistent rumours back then that he had been crazy about one of the princesses he knew in his youth, but the Reverend later became convinced that his true passion had always been for keeping secrets, both state and private. In this way, the General had managed to build his own business in the financial security system and enjoyed favoured access to enterprises whose doors were not open to the common man. However, no special woman nor 'Madonna and child' had ever appeared in his entourage.

The Reverend waited patiently for an explanation for his cousin's sudden appearance at Kew Gardens, his fascination focused on what his real motives might be as a custodian of high-ranking interests. As for the General, the stroll reminded him of crossing the 'death strip' that had existed between East and West Berlin from 1961 to 1989 and had attested, for more than a quarter of a century, to the fact that the marking of borders on a map leads to the emergence of hidden battlefields not shown on any modern topographical charts. Meanwhile, they had arrived at the Minka House, which was surrounded by a unique bamboo garden covering several dozen square metres and containing 1,200 species from China, Japan, the Himalayas, and the United States. At the entrance to the Bamboo Garden, they were met by the medicinal, fan-shaped leaves of a 'living fossil' (*Ginkgo biloba*). The Reverend let out a sigh of relief and closed his parasol as they reached the shade of the House and sat down on a bench. Minka became their island of recuperation as the General came to his point.

'I merely wanted to warn you: New Babylon's current Transition to an updated version involves a rather different protocol from the previous iterations.'

'Different in what way?'

'Control over global security has been put in the hands of a human being for seven days.'

'Hmmm – never a dull moment when you're around!'

'Patience is all I ask of you until the machine moves over to the new variant. The algorithms for the Transition were prescribed many years ago and took account of rates of growth of threats in the global world that can change within the course of a week. As a self-taught system, machine intelligence knows its own limitations.'

The Reverend was listening attentively. 'You mean to say that even as we stand here chatting about the fate of the world, machine intelligence is continuing to learn new things?' he pondered thoughtfully. 'Remind me, my dear, how is the global balance of interests maintained during a Transition?'

The General chuckled. He knew the Reverend had now grasped the essence of what he was saying.

'Just a week then. No one is more patient than the Church, as you know. But, mark you, I know that any experiment is a big risk.'

'The computations made during the Transition have never failed yet.'

'General, you are creating a computerised man-God. Tell me honestly, doesn't it frighten you a little too – the idea of an intelligence that might one day turn into a deity or everlasting dictator whose power over the earth is limitless? If something happens in the outside world, I will not enable the rewriting of the brand-new story that is to take place under the influence of your exceptional circumstances.'

'Gaining power over time is the farthest thing from your mind. By studying the world around us, New Babylon is trying to uncover new threats, Your Grace. It is important to identify and provide due warning about errors that could be linked to threats to many human lives. I am more concerned about manifestations of a different kind.'

'Warning people about a scandal like SKYNET[5] is in the best interests of global security.'

'As you may remember, Bruce Schneier[6] had a tough time of it when he had to explain the price of Google's mistake. He was forced to fend off attacks from the press because a vital military programme shut down.'

A light breeze ruffled the tops of the trees. It started to cool down a little. The Reverend was delighted.

'Everything in the world is tranquil. Splendid! Still not even a hint of a cloud in the sky. The only ordeal we now have to face is the walk back to the gates of the gardens on a hot day. Did your New Babylon does not give any hint about the real state of affairs in the world?'

'Lines from Lewis Carroll's poetry help me to become aware of new aspects of the rules of life. What are you reading at the moment?'

'The *Rubáiyát of Omar Khayyám*. The Persian astronomer was the first to put forward solutions to quadratic algebraic equations, thereby creating the most accurate calendar of all, one that is still used today. Those rules may prove to be of use to you in the near future. Just imagine it – the emergence of a competitor who is invisible to the global security system!'

'It's my duty to give you an honest warning about the main problem in the development of New Babylon that we are

---

[5] A US National Security Agency programme that performs machine analysis on communications data to extract information about possible terror suspects.

[6] An American cryptographer, computer security specialist, and author of several books on security, cryptography, and cybersecurity.

currently working to solve. What matters is being able to take changes in other non-linear environments into account; for instance, humanity's new living conditions, our impact on the biosphere…'

'The love of God has not changed in the last couple of thousand years.'

'I wouldn't argue with you, Your Grace.'

'Today has turned out to be a wonderful opportunity for building bridges, General.'

In excellent spirits, the cousins set off towards the exit. A contented silence fell over them as they strolled through the Orangery towards Elizabeth Gate. On the other side of the railings, a young man stood waiting for the Reverend, accompanied by a bevy of silver-coated Italian greyhounds, whose slender necks were adorned with elegant dog collars bearing medals. They were their master's pride and joy, having been a gift from Pope Francis.

'There was one call for you, Your Grace. You've been invited to a presentation by Augustin Hoffman that is to be unveiled among the thermal waters, glaciers, and volcanoes of Iceland.' The dog walker bowed politely, gesturing for them to go through the gates first. The Reverend handed him the parasol and steered the General forward.

The General found his cousin's choice of assistant rather surprising. The dog walker hardly looked like the sort of person with whom he usually associated. He had the olive skin of a Mediterranean, employed mannered gestures, displayed a pierced earlobe and was dressed in a shiny suit. He resembled to him a talented chancer who had yet to acquire a proper sense of the power of money. How exactly had this young Count of St Germain got his feet under the table? *It does seem utterly reckless of him to entrust his beloved dogs to this fellow*, he thought. Neither had the new sartorial details of the Reverend's appearance escaped his notice: the silk handkerchief with Versace patterns he used to wipe his face; the parasol; the sandals he was now carrying. The General was inclined to ascribe all these changes in appearance and behaviour to the arrival of this young servant in His Grace's entourage.

'You are aware, no doubt, of my fondness for dogs?' the Reverend probed. 'I've been informed that Her Majesty the Queen has ordered that all of them must undergo check-ups.'

The General chuckled. 'The RSPCA has announced that all household pets must be inspected for the presence of allergens. It's a perfectly normal security measure. You have nothing to worry about – your Italian greyhounds are the most famous in the city.'

'May I pass on the news about the government inspection of my canine companions?'

'Of course! You can tell all the dog lovers and whomever else you see fit,' the General laughed. 'What's more, the information is going to be officially published today. I've heard more than enough about a new nanny for your dogs, Reverend, not to mention your public jaunts through the park. Your little piglet looks marvellous against the backdrop of Dog Park.' He turned slightly towards the newcomer. 'So, this is the fellow who inspired you to come up with that quaint idea about "the gentleman who doesn't pay the rent"?'

A death strip had once again been formed between the cousins, who exchanged bows and went their separate ways. The General set off towards picturesque St Anne's Church, where the artist Thomas Gainsborough was buried, while the Reverend, accompanied by the dog walker and the greyhounds, headed towards the river. The long-awaited full tide was coming in.

TRANSITION KEEPER

'Everything in one symbol. Hurry!'

All the technical devices in the house turned themselves on silently and simultaneously. A plethora of LEDs of various colours began flickering busily as their power supplies were activated. Now she could maintain a supply of electricity without having to make any extra effort.

TRANSITION KEEPER took in the TV news. She didn't need so much as to flick through the endless news channels to be able to work out in advance all the mathematical algorithms for sporting events, the outcome of elections in a host of democratic countries, or even the style and colour of the skirts worn by the presenters and their guests in the TV studios. Her consciousness was filled with reams of the symbolic shapes of Piero Manzoni's 'Achrome'[7] *and the experiments of the Lucio Fontana*[8] *school of the 1940s and 1950s: innumerable images with whose help she had learnt a multitude of new symbolic data values. Billions of megabytes of artistic moulds – values and symbols – were*

---

[7] A work of art by Piero Manzoni, a follower of Lucio Fontana known for his experiments with colouring materials and inflatable membranes, whose famous works include a mechanical sculpture of an animal levitating in a stream of air and a 'magic pedestal', ascending to which everyone becomes a work of art.

[8] Author of the 'Manifesto Blanco', which emphasised the importance of new technologies as they pertained to the arts, the integration of art and science, and the exploitation of modern mass media, radio, and television.

identified, as though she had become part of Tomaso Poggio's[9] instant image recognition programme. For each request, TRANSITION KEEPER had several alternative answers, each associated with a geographical place, time, and digital calculation, but she required one true answer to the question before the Transition programme was completed.

TRANSITION KEEPER opened the door to a garage that for many years had housed an three exclusive retro cars and discovered an exclusive model similar to a Tatra 77, the first aerodynamic construction by the Austrian engineer Paul Gerain, who was also the first to prove that a streamlined shape affected the speed and manoeuvrability of road vehicles. The car opened its doors, fastened the seatbelt, displayed the route and turned on the engine. Just like Gary F. Marcus's 'auto-pilot', TRANSITION KEEPER was transformed into a mechanism that could control multiple transport flows moving around the highways of Europe. Boom barriers opened to grant her access, and other vehicles moved aside to let her through traffic jams. All the traffic lights turned green.

---

[9] A professor with the Laboratory of Computer Science and AI at Massachusetts Institute of Technology, and the creator of a computer programme capable of competing in speed with a person in a specific field via 'instant recognition'.

The Secret Room, London

A newsflash flitted across the top and bottom of the big screen – *No active news. Attention. TRANSITION* – in the middle of which appeared a line from an English poem, followed by the words *I shall be with you and within you. I shall love both your darkness and your light.*

It was like some sort of joke.

The General opened a window containing *The Washington Post*'s latest straplines:

China's Armed Forces have stepped up their exercises involving the use of bombers

In the UK, Boris Johnson has returned to the role of Prime Minister

The president of Russia has drawn level with the president of Ukraine in popular support. The two countries presidents have the backing of more than 70% of the electorate

Angela Merkel has met the Dalai Lama, having expressed a desire to stay on as head of the government until 2021 and not stand as a candidate for the Bundestag

Blowing-up of a car containing a well-known journalist in the capital city.

He switched over to the forecasts of international analytical agencies but soon stopped what he was doing. *I shall be with you and within you*, he repeated to himself. It sounded like something one might expect to hear from a wandering minstrel rather than an artificial intelligence machine as sophisticated as New Babylon. When he had examined the message from the machine on the morning of the second day, there had been only one question on his mind: Why did a supercomputer tasked with looking after global security feel the need to conclude its monologue with a line of Lewis Carroll verse and a poetic trick?

It was therefore in a battle-ready state of mind that the General left his ivory tower and headed for Hatchard's bookshop. He had chosen an Austin F black cab so that he could get around London without attracting unwanted attention. His chauffeur, Richard, resembled the CEO of the Virgin Group – a happy circumstance that had given the General a soft spot for him, who had always let him come to work without a tie throughout his many years of service.

After Richard stopped the car on the corner of Green Park, the General set off on foot from the former favourite duelling site of English aristocrats towards Piccadilly and the fountain with the dancing Eros made of a dark aluminium alloy. For him, the area had for a long time meant Robert Baker Street. In 1612, Baker bought some of the land and built Piccadilly Hall, earning a fortune by selling fashionable 'Piccadilly' neckwear. The General adored the daily hubbub of London's main commercial artery. He turned into the grey stone passageway of The Ritz, passing the delicatessen and chocolatiers Fortnum & Mason, which had for four centuries supplied fine foods and sweet treats to the Royal Court and featured a toy apiary on its roof. It could be seen from the opposite side of the road, where Bentley & Skinner, which sold exquisite antiquarian and silver jewellery, and Burlington House, once home to nine Royal Scientific communities, could also be found.

Before he reached Piccadilly's countless arcades, however, he stepped into the oldest bookshop in London, which for centuries had enjoyed royal patronage – a privilege confirmed by a modest plaque on the wall to the right of the entrance: *By Appointment to H.R.H. The Duke of Edinburgh & The Prince of Wales were patrons of this Bookseller.* Its multilevel interior was organised around a central staircase, on which the General spotted a well-known author and her publisher among the rank-and-file lovers of books making their way up and down the wooden steps. The biggest attraction at Hatchards was the collection of signed editions by some of the greatest names in world literature.

What the General loved about the hustle and bustle of this outgoing age were its classical objects and artworks. In the circles of today's young elites, he might have been considered odd – perhaps even something of a renegade – on account of his delight in browsing rare volumes and artefacts, but here he could chat unreservedly about the latest acquisitions to any of the other aficionados on the premises.

Today, however, he did not walk down to the Rare Books but went straight upstairs to the Poetry section. Beside the shelves of verse, he caught sight of his old acquaintance wearing his trademark impertinent half-smile.

'Is this what you're looking for by any chance?'

Without taking his frank gaze off the General for an instant, his erstwhile associate was holding out an anthology containing works by Matsuo Bashō, Federico García Lorca, and W.B. Yeats.

And, of course, An Agony in Eight Fits.

'Simon! I can't say it fills me with pleasure to see you surrounded by the works of Golding, Greene, and Brodsky. Perhaps you have come to the wrong shop?'

Simon impudently screwed up his eyes. 'I'm in exactly the right place. I have decided to appeal for help in person, General. Today is the end of our Cold War.' He repeated the news from that morning's newspaper. An American initiative had brought to an end the agreement between the USSR and USA – signed in Washington on 8th December 1987, a year after the accident at the Chernobyl nuclear power plant – to liquidate medium- and short-range missiles.

'So now you're a peacemaker? How do you like that! And there was I thinking you were working on some secret project at DARPA! Have you come up with something more interesting than the IP protocol and GPS?'

'The ARPANET[10] and Project 5719 are pretty outmoded nowadays. The matter I want to talk about requires a New Babylon.'

'You've decided to sign up as an admirer of the machine again?'

'The reason has to do with TRANSITION KEEPER. The latest Transition was announced by your machine yesterday, right? Do you know the reason?'

'Wars are no longer waged by separate states but by individual militias, and the boundaries of conflicts are tightly interwoven with the ordinary world. In the past, legal and societal

---

[10] The first wide-area, packet-switching network with distributed control and the first network to implement the TCP/IP protocol suite, whose dual technologies became the technological foundation of the Internet.

laws did not apply to the actions of states.' The General handed him a black watch. 'What on earth happened to make you appeal to me for help? Has someone started the Third World War? Why should you care about TRANSITION KEEPER now, ten years down the line?'

'I included a poetic trick in the term "supercomputer", General. The TRANSITION KEEPER programme would not have been possible without this option.'

'So that's what it is … I was utterly convinced that you had finished your military career and would never go back to the kind of grand concerns you and I once worked on.'

'I used to kill time writing poetry, but I've given that up. Please hear me out. It was I who set the machine a task whereby it had to quote a line of verse in the event that it launched the TRANSITION KEEPER programme. You are the only person I would like to make peace with right now, General. That's why I'm here.'

'And you came here to confess as much to me?' The General took the anthology from Simon's outstretched hands.

'I pose no threat to you. I am currently working on professional downshifting at Reporters Without Borders, a non-governmental organisation that looks into freedom of information issues.'

'Paragraph nineteen of the Universal Declaration of Human Rights? Well then, Simon, let's concern ourselves with your affairs. Think of it as a mark of our long-standing friendly relations. I know a place not far from here where we can speak freely. I haven't looked in on Maison Assouline for quite a while.'

EARLIER – THE GENERAL

The tests in the General's laboratory had begun in the summer of 1997. A year before, three of the world's leading scientists – the cyberneticist Ervin László, the psychiatrist Stanislav Grof, and the linguist Peter Russell – were beginning their dialogue[11] about a looming catastrophe. Their research was classified and ongoing. The General, having earned himself an impeccable reputation among both the powers that be and his friends, had by that time decided to busy himself with some technological developments of his own in the field of global security systems. He had immediately caught the interest of a host of governmental and non-governmental organisations, creating a private IT company with a team of developers from all over the world who professed a desire to warn the planet of crises, threats, and disasters.

The General had proposed that they adopt a somewhat different approach from that of the secret War Rooms built in the United States after the Cuban Missile Crisis. The US federal government had at that time begun pouring money into university research programmes, since it was felt that wide-ranging support of science would encourage military breakthroughs. That year, President Eisenhower founded the Defense Advanced Research Projects Agency (DARPA).[12] This was the golden age of

---

[11] See The Consciousness Revolution: A Transatlantic Dialogue (Element Books, 1999).

[12] An agency of the United States Department of Defense

artificial intelligence, with studies that explored its ability to understand natural language, music created by computers, expert systems, and video games such as Spacewar. The creation of the Stanford Artificial Intelligence Laboratory (SAIL)[13] and the coming into being of such initiatives and principles as open-source software and network neutrality had laid the groundwork for an optimistic outlook on AI.

The General's intention was to create a supercomputer that could accumulate various kinds of input data and conduct analyses, making predictions more quickly than any human and giving recommendations on which threats to warn the public about. He believed in a simple and elegant open-code solution that contained an idea he had clung to ever since he was a young man. To disarm an aggressor, what you had to do was stop them from believing that their own aggressive actions were going to succeed. To do this, there was no need to meddle in conflicts in the traditional sense through shows of strength. All that was required was to include the aggressor in a communications system that would alter their inner beliefs and values to render harmless any real threat that was developing and maintain equilibrium.

In fairness, it should be said that at one stage the Reverend had provided an invaluable service to the General when he gave him comprehensive descriptions of all the known conflicts that had taken place around the world, which he had gleaned from the Bible and the history of Christianity. In fact, one of the General's employees had suggested that the supercomputer ought to be

---

responsible for the development of emerging technologies for use by the military.
[13] See Professor John McCarthy, 'What is AI? / Basic Questions'. http:// jmc.stanford.edu/artificial-intelligence/what-is-ai/index.html, accessed 10 July 2020.

given its biblical name of New Babylon. The General had liked the idea. He had found out in advance that Simon had no in-depth knowledge of the texts of the Old and New Testaments and that his personal story had begun with his flight from East Germany to New England. *Simon probably isn't even his real name*, the General had thought as he studied the youthful new recruit before him, who turned out to be a sharp-tongued, erudite, and fearless lad from a poor family. Their first conversation had been memorable.

'So, you're Simon – the man with the golden ears? I advise you to study not only the Bible but also the Koran and the Buddhist source texts of the *Trikaya*.' The General found himself smiling. 'I've heard about your ideas.'

'I am familiar with the Koran and Buddhist sources and have just finished the foundational Chinese work. Confucianism will soon be recognised as one of the official world doctrines.'

The General had admired Simon's eagerness to solve problems. 'And this is the most dramatic aspect, one that requires a little thought. What language will the rival AI speak?'

'How will New Babylon find out about its own existence?' Simon had waited till he was sure that the General appreciated his reply before continuing. 'I could improve this concept.'

'New Babylon does not meddle with reality. That could be its Achilles' heel.'

'Might I take up just a few minutes of your time?' Simon smiled.

Piccadilly, London

Simon and the General left Hatchards and wove their way through the hustle of Piccadilly to Maison Assouline and a place of refuge from the latest trends in high fashion, design, and travel. The oasis in the middle of the metropolis was only a short walk from the bookseller and several hundred yards from St James's Church, the last resting place of gentlemen-in-waiting and physicians to the aristocracy.

'Where are you staying?' the General asked.

'At the Wellington guest house in Rochester Row. I arrived yesterday.'

'Still being true to yourself, I see. On the fringes, near a railway station…'

'It's more that I'm being true to my habits. You can spot changes quickly from the edges, no?'

'And there I was thinking Rochester Row was a place to relax for the modern man who can't get used to life in London, New York, and Berlin. There are plenty of places to drink beer, but finding a pleasant spot for lunch for two is rather tricky.'

Their casual chit-chat had brought them to the doors of their destination, which stood on the site of a former bank. A notice beside the entrance announced the layout:

2nd floor – Cabinet de Curiosités. Meeting Rooms 1st floor – Rare & Vintage Books
Ground floor – Books & Gifts. Swan Bar

The dining area was appointed to give aesthetic delight. There were mirrors faded by time, panelled walls, copies of Roman bas-reliefs, shelves of curios, and a unique collection of photo albums.

Cocktails, hot meals, and drinks could be ordered at the bar at any time of the day or night. The clock on the wall showed the correct time twice a day.

'Shall we order something for old times' sake before we head upstairs?' the General suggested. 'Two glasses of whiskey – Midleton Green Spot,' he told the waiter.

Simon was pleased. Evidently, the General was willing to have a more frank and in-depth conversation with him.

After they had drained their glasses, the cousins went up to the second floor via a staircase concealed in a recess. The Meeting Rooms at Maison Assouline, hidden from the view of ordinary visitors, were furnished with leather armchairs from a former age, a sculpture of a pining Apollo, and wood-framed screens with patterns of soft roses on the fabric. When the light fell on the red-headed Simon's face, his once mischievous features took on a mature look, acquiring a resemblance to the 'rebellious' Jesus by Luis de Morales, a painter dubbed 'El Divino' by his contemporaries because of his attention to sacred subjects.

When the drinks arrived, the two men raised their glasses without uttering a word, inwardly recalling the early days of their friendship when their first few meetings had blossomed into heated discussions, whereupon the office would quickly empty save for the two of them. The ambience at Maison Assouline made the General nostalgic for a vanished era. Some time ago, he had taken an interest in high fashion, made the acquaintance of some of those who created it and even attended several parties. In the past, there had always been plenty of guests, and it had become immediately apparent to him that all the clients had very different reasons for turning their attention to the industry. Some attended the fashion shows to practise bodily elegance and cultivate their passion for beauty, while others simply liked to acquire and collect beautiful things. His own personal fascination for the fashion and design business at Assouline had been about observing those who wore the clothes of the great designers, the correctness of whose lines and curves and the quality of whose garments were of great importance. The moment they were left alone, the General was the first to return to the conversation they had broken off beside the bookshelves.

'Do you remember, Simon? Ten years ago, you convinced me that a woman could be one of the Transition scripts for New Babylon. This was necessary in order for the machine to take account of every possible single error that can occur in the world of people. It was your idea to suggest a woman as a TRANSITION KEEPER programme.'

'Indeed – I insisted on it!'

'I.introduced the "Rapid Automatic Transition" protected programmeearlier,' replied the General.

'The threat to TRANSITION KEEPER may come from a real opponent of New Babylon at any time.'

'And who could this real opponent be?'

'Augustin Hoffman. I'm sure this could prove to be vitally important information for your friends in international journalists' associations – and indeed for any observers.'

EARLIER – SIMON

A few days after the idea for a 'Rapid Automatic Transition' of the machine from its old programme was approved, Simon had gone to see the General for a working meeting.

'In order for New Babylon to remain in *perpetuum mobile*,[14] A transition is required: a period in which the machine fills itself up with algorithms based on new data from other systems, he announced, having taken the floor. 'The supercomputer is not perfect. It uses only the data that have been entered into the statistical database. The Transition is the period in which the machine acquires new information and knowledge about the outside world and automatically makes adjustments to the source code corresponding to the rapidly changing situation.'

The General unhurriedly turned away from a programme monitoring the payment of taxes by rapidly growing companies. 'So you are proposing that *perpetuum mobile* has to do with a self-learning system? The idea of such a machine is not new. What matters is how it will obtain new ideas about life and mankind.'

'The impact of the human factor – that value is not present among the machine's set of coefficients, indices, and algorithms.

---

[14] A hypothetical machine that can do work indefinitely without an energy source. In 2017, new states of matter, 'time crystals', were discovered, in which the component atoms are in continual repetitive motion at a sub-microscopic level, thus satisfying the literal definition of 'perpetual motion'.

Have a think about Omar Khayyám's book on how to make a human life invulnerable, or it might not be able to withstand competition from the machine world.' Simon placed a terracotta figurine on the desk in front of the General. 'I have solved the problem of *perpetuum mobile* with a temporal crystal. The woman will be more likely to find the lost music and mathematics in a crisis situation.' He triumphantly declaimed lines from Ovid's *Amores*:

> *And he created a person – such a woman*
> *the world had never seen – and he loved his creation.*

The General began examining the figurine, which appeared to be an original work. By the looks of it, it must have cost a small fortune. The eye sockets were embedded with deep purple gemstones, and on its head was that ancient symbol of feminine power: an upturned crescent moon.

'Are you proposing to give the female sex all the rights of control over the global security and threat alert system?'

'For the duration of one of the Transitions, yes.'

'A backup for artificial intelligence in a crisis situation,' pondered the General, rotating the figurine in his hands.

Simon went on thinking out loud. 'Women and men have different pain thresholds. In women, they are far lower. And then there are the emotional, hormonal, and other differences ... women's empathy is far better developed than that of the average man. Will it not interfere with the machine to have to subject matters of progeny to mathematical calculations? That sphere could be sold off to big computing too.'

'We shouldn't forget the legend of Samson and his hair, according to which the Judean lost all his warrior strength after falling in love with the avaricious Delilah, who cut off his mythic locks while he was sleeping ... but you know, Simon, I think I'm willing to agree to this solution. Man don't experience the progeny pain. Let the machine itself choose the time, the place, and the subject's name within the seven days of the Transition.'

'I agree. The woman is more likely than the man to identify discrepancies and weak spots in the machine's programme.'

After their conversation, the General invited Simon to join him for a glass of wine at a pub beside the Thames. They walked along the river to The Royal Barge, where they sat at a table by the window overlooking the water.

'Why have you never told me who your parents are, who your family is?'

'Allow me to keep my name a secret,' he replied evenly. 'Who brought you up?'

'My uncle tried to raise me, but it must be said he did a pretty bad job. I ran away – from him and Eastern Europe.'

'I won't ask about your relationships with women ...'

'Why not? I can be frank with you.'

The General gave a fatherly chuckle. 'It's a trifling matter, Simon. You love them, women.'

'I don't believe in happiness, General, merely in the anticipation of it.'

They lingered at the pub until dusk, admiring the canoeists zigzagging along the river before draining their glasses. By the end of the weekend, the General had asked Simon to take charge of his laboratory. He needed a witness for New Babylon's rebirth, and he had found one. *Everyone may have a secret*, he thought, shaking the young man's hand.

The General had gathered what few details he could find out about Simon's life. His uncle had fled from the site of a major disaster in the USSR to be with the woman he loved in East Germany. As a result, a huge number of people had died, and the world had learned of the biggest man-made catastrophe of the previous century. The most likely scenario was that the Federal Intelligence Service had found out about it from Simon's uncle.

As it turned out, however, the General had chosen very wisely; Simon coped admirably with the assignments given to him. He had a talent for imbuing his ideas with special meaning and telling everyone about them, seeming to fill the space around him with a seething energy. The General valued him for the ideas he contributed to the development process, from his very first act of vandalism – furnishing the machine with a checklist for the ability to tell jokes – to his fundamental provocation: launching the TRANSITION KEEPER programme by using a female subject in the event of 'exceptional circumstances' to identify rapid threats. Over time, Simon became the General's regular conversation partner at The Royal Barge at weekends. His erudition went far beyond the amusing fables and elegant tall tales that he was forever telling in the lab, some of which concerned facts of which even the General was unaware.

Simon knew a great many interesting things about Soviet cosmonauts, the days of the Cold War, the talks that were held between the USSR and West Germany, and even the level to which the water fell before the explosion in the Chernobyl nuclear reactor.

They had remained friends until the latter simply disappeared one day without a word of explanation. At first, the General had thought there must be a woman on the scene. In any event, he made no attempt to go looking for him. From the moment he vanished from the secret lab, Simon had never shown up at any of the serious agencies that worked in the field of AI.

Not at the US research laboratory at MIT; nor at Lockheed Martin; Northrop Grumman; nor Boeing – all of which might have been capable of competing with his invention. The General had concluded that Simon no longer posed a threat; his glory days had irrevocably come to an end. And so, he had lost interest in his talented former employee until the two of them crossed paths in the Poetry department of a London bookshop.

Piccadilly, London

Simon handed the General a sheet of paper folded into containing a list of names. 'It shows the data of all the people who have received earrings as a bonus in a game called Dresses and invited to the future event in Island,' he told him. The General did not see in it the name of the 'nanny' dogs of Reverend.

'I see their addresses and likely future movements are also stated,' he noted. 'New Babylon is not monitoring an organisation but a rank-and-file populist – Augustin Hoffman! It would take a brave person to try to infringe on a concept on the scale of New Babylon's mission!'

'But let me get one thing straight! I have never had, nor do I currently have, any enemies – apart, perhaps, from that much-hyped company Cambridge Analytica that caused a stir by introducing the new rules of the game in political rivalry.'

'I wonder what would take New Babylon's place if the programme should fail. In all likelihood, it would be SpiNNaker,[15] the technology recently launched by scientists at MIT, which models the functioning of the brain's neural networks. Let's cast our minds back. You're suggesting that the presentation in Iceland has something to do with this?' Simon

---

[15] Spiking Neural Network Architecture: a massively parallel, manycore supercomputer architecture used in simulating the human brain. https://www.computer.org/csdl/magazine/co/2015/10/mco2015100006/13RuxD qSc2*Ali Blank*

pressed.

The General was thinking of how this was the second time in 24 hours that the little-known name of Augustin Hoffman and his presentation in Iceland had been sounded. He was sure that Hoffman was not connected to either of his namesakes – neither the professor and theoretician of multi-communication nor the director of the Pentagon, nor the photographer of Hitler. While spending time reading through New Babylon's reports in the Secret Room, he also felt sure that he knew the world better than Hoffman. *In that case, TRANSITION KEEPER won't have any trouble calculating a hidden mass political threat stemming from his new game – if such a threat even exists,* he thought. 'You're not much good as a psychologist, Simon,' he teased. 'Go on, tell me more about Hoffman! You're the man who has the data on him.'

Simon walked over from the fabric of the screen, finishing his scotch. The General was asking him to make a proper pitch.

'Augustin Hoffman grew up in communist Eastern Europe just like me. He was neither a neurophysiologist nor a nuclear physicist. He made money by playing the piano there until he got married, and he married well. He also used to love saying that life was full of fabrications.'

'You don't seem to have any proof, only suspicions, the General thought aloud. 'I am going to tell you about something of which I am certain, Simon. Hoffman's financial resources would scarcely be sufficient for carrying out expensive experiments like the LIGO[16] experiment conducted by Kip

---

[16] A large-scale physics experiment and observatory to detect cosmic gravitational waves and time and space distortions predicted by Einstein in 1916. At a cost of $365 million, it is one of the most expensive projects funded by the National Science Foundation in the United States.

Thorne.'[17] The General frowned as he gave the matter some thought. Hoffman's mobile app had only caught New Babylon's eye because the product had quickly become popular during the crisis in the Middle East, but the General had not ascribed any great significance to such an efficient instrument for holding teenagers in its thrall. Needless to say, he was aware that Hoffman's stock was rising in the US market. However, his attention had been caught by a different company, one that was incomprehensible and inaccessible to those who loved electronic music, mobile apps like Dresses, and synthetic desserts. There was no trace of anything dangerous in Hoffman's actions. His activities to date have never been linked to any hacking attacks nor any scandals regarding information, espionage, or significant scientific discoveries. Surely, he, the General, could not have missed anything important?

By that time, the epicentre of high fashion had moved from secret offices, private parties, and stylish studios to the online world. The sites at houses in the suburbs – where until new collections by the leading designers had been put on show – had closed because imitation *haute couture* clothes could now be bought online as a result of the success of the Dresses game. Hoffman had concentrated on a topic far removed from global security, and his product had been integrated with manifold cloud services. The game, which consisted of users of the mobile app finding friends wearing the same outfits as them in public places, had quickly become popular, in the course of which people were encouraged to expand their circle of contacts through discounted clothes in the shops. The app has been downloaded millions of times.

---

[17] One of the world's leading experts on the astrophysical implications of Einstein's general theory of relativity and a scientific consultant to Christopher Nolan's film *Interstellar*.

There was a long pause in their discussion.

'I won't be revealing any secrets if I tell you that such a threat as Hoffman's power over teenagers is included in New Babylon's monitoring programme,' the General confidently declared, who had remained loyal and solitary in his investigations into the laws of the system he had brought into being. 'As you well know, non-military organisations do not have such resources. Nowadays, wars can be started by a single developer through a mobile app, using a database. It doesn't look when it compiled the list as though the programme applied a formula from the server and academic laboratory of the large Collider[18] at CERN,' he observed, his brow furrowed. 'You need to look at the list of guests from the Hoffman presentation and cross-check it against anyone who may have set about solving highly complex tasks in the field of IT security. Hoffman may have had someone helping him.' He rose from his seat.

The two men left the private rooms on the upper floor and walked down to the main dining area of Maison Assouline. There're some urgent problems to solve.

'You don't believe my assumption. Forgive me, General, there's one other thing I wanted to ask you. Do you have any news of Margaret?'

The General rolled his eyes playfully as some long-forgotten mirages came back to him, recalling the last time he had visited Maison Assouline with her many years ago. 'I haven't heard a word from her for many moons. Aren't you asking rather too many questions for a ten-year reunion?' He was glad that the half-darkness of the staircase hid the expression on his face. In

---

[18] The world's largest and highest-energy particle collider, a collaboration between over 10,000 scientists and hundreds of universities and laboratories in more than 100 countries, is located in a tunnel beneath the French-Swiss border near Geneva.

Swan Bar, he had ordered her a cocktail called 'Pierre Cardin' and one for himself called 'Frida Kahlo'. While they were waiting for them to arrive, Margaret had browsed through some albums of rare objects laid out on special stands, using the synthetic white gloves guests were required to put on before touching the pages. The first thing that caught the General's eye now, from up on the second-floor balcony, was that very same album, *The Impossible Collection of Cigars and Wine*, in the centre of the hall. It looked to him as though no one else had handled those pages in all the intervening years.

When the two men found themselves back in noisy Piccadilly, the General headed towards his black cab. Simon took in his broad, straight back. *I ought to give him credit for his strong will and profound knowledge of people*, he thought. The General's internal logic, unknown to anyone, invariably found a way around snares and traps. How many times had Simon witnessed his far-sightedness and wondered whether it was intuition or he was getting clues from the supercomputer? Therein lay the great strength of their collaboration, one that neither time nor the secrets they kept from one another had destroyed. But today the General remained a silent enigma to him, an unsolved question to which he was still seeking an answer.

After their leave-taking on London's commercial artery, Simon set off on foot towards one of Christopher Wren's creations, the Church of St Stephen Walbrook, which was considered one of the most beautiful churches in the city. Thanks to the unique asymmetrical construction technique adopted by its architect, it resembled an alluring woman: modest on the outside; and luxurious on the inside. Meanwhile, the General was heading for the British Museum. He needed to find a man whose skills and knowledge he considered to be on a par with the talents of

Sir Hans Sloane, who had replaced Sir Isaac Newton as president of the British Museum Society. The Society had engaged in 'experimental philosophy' with the aim of demonstrating the scientific principles that might explain the laws of nature. Failing to find him, he made straightaway for the museum's private hall, passing through gates made of four types of marble, where a new exhibition was being prepared that was dedicated to the Middle Ages. Several metres above the heads of the visitors, a caretaker was cleaning depictions of the saints on the wooden altar of St Margaret, who was executed for refusing to forswear Christianity. There was a dragon entwined around her legs.

'I am pleased to see that noble bare head of yours, Taylor. I have an urgent question for you, the General called out to him.

The caretaker turned around. To the General's surprise, however, he was not the man he had been looking for at all.

'Greetings, General. Taylor isn't here.' The stranger passed his brush delicately across the face of Margaret. 'In my experience, the key thing is where the natural light would fall on the face. Taylor asked me to tell you, General, about the portrait hidden under Gainsborough's painting, news the museum hesitated to make public for a long time. Whose portrait do you think Gainsborough concealed?' He paused for effect while the General regarded him quizzically. 'His own mother's!'

'For your information, shadows are sometimes far more expressive. Someone is interested in the interactive map of the medieval world created on thirty sheets,' the General surmised.

Finding himself inside the black cab once again, he felt overcome by the exhausting events of the day. 'Let's go back to the Secret Room, Richard. I didn't find Taylor. Simon was not wrong. Someone, or something, is threatening TRANSITION KEEPER. The meeting will happen on neutral waters as usual. Find out the place and time!'

DAY TWO

Carinthia, Austria

The glint of the water's smooth surface at the foot of the stone faces of the Alps, the spires of the little brick churches surrounded by grazing cows, and the main roads arrowing across the landscape created a special rhythm for a passenger travelling by high-speed train from Vienna. Ten-year-old Alice arrived in the Drau Valley in provincial Austria with a small suitcase containing a change of clothes, some earphones, a toothbrush, a purse, and a book. The train stopped at a small railway station called Spital Millstadt, scattered around which were little villages like handfuls of seeds. She came quickly on foot to the guest house in Seeboden on Millstadt See, a tiny place whose German name means 'Lake Bottom'. The biggest tourist attraction in the Drau Valley was without question its five major lakes: Wörthersee; Millstätter See; Ossiacher See; Faaker See; and Lake Klopein; as well as 1,270 small lagoons, which served as the sources of half the rivers in Italy and provided Austria's water supply.

Alice's hair was its natural colour save for its green tips. She played her favourite game: trying to recall all the facts she knew about Carinthia. However, she could only remember two things. In 2008, a regional law had been passed banning the construction of minarets; one of its authors, a Member of Parliament representing the Austrian People's Party and the Alliance for the Future of Austria, was later exposed as having ties to Saddam Hussein and Colonel Gaddafi. The second thing was that one of the villages, Rafting, was the birthplace of the man who wrote *The Thermodynamics of Real Processes*. The local myths and secrets didn't count as real.

Alice only ever took one book with her when she went travelling. This time it was *The Veritable Records of the Manchus*, but she hadn't read a single line of it.

The guest house was located on top of a windswept hill covered with pine trees. At its foot lay the tranquil waters of Millstätter See.

Lady Swan, took possession of the house. Though she did not usually have guests to stay, she had made an exception for her niece and her nanny on their first visit to Carinthia. Alice had moved into a room on the top floor known as 'The Nest', while Nanny took the downstairs guest room. Lady Swan's living quarters took up the entire first floor of the guest house, including the terrace. While Nanny was visiting all the usual places on a well-trodden route around Seeboden – the beach, the local bakery – Alice and the landlady had lain in deckchairs in the garden and read the clouds, for Lady Swan, like Alice herself, had mastered this remarkable skill. Then, when the sky was clear, they sheltered from the intense heat and ultraviolet rays under some wisteria, lazing and chatting. That was how the shared secret between them had come into being.

'Lady Swan, how does the sky choose who to talk to?'

'The sky only speaks to those who help others stay alive.'

'The main thing to remember is that you should only tell a secret to someone who can keep it, Lady Swan.'

'The main thing to remember about a secret is to find an object, put it in a hole in the ground and cover it carefully with glass, my little bird. I'm going to offer you something a little more interesting. Let us create a hiding place for us to keep secrets in. I will put a key to the house there. If anything should happen, you will always be able to come back and stay here. If I ever need you here quickly, I'll send you a parcel.'

On her way to the house, Alice encountered no one, other than a red deer munching on some red huckleberry – and she considered this brush with a wild animal a good omen. Then she noticed the pleasant scent of perfume in the air and hid. From her hiding place, she saw the backs of an Asian woman and a man standing on the path. *These are strange-looking characters*, she thought. Alice peered out cautiously from behind the wisteria, trying to work out who these new protagonists were. She was too far away to decipher the meaning of the carefully drawn tattoo on the woman's body but close enough to be able to add to their portrait as they continued their walk towards the alpine stream.

Alice slipped unnoticed into the garden. Like one of the guide suitcases for the blind developed by IBM, a huge dragonfly led her down the path, which was lined with daisies and pansies. She was entirely ignorant of the fact that her every move through the streets was being tracked.

The house looked firmly under lock and key. The shutters on the ground floor were closed. Its hedgerow formed part of the renowned gardens surrounding it, whose layout could easily be grasped by passers-by: the lawns; the brightly coloured highlights of the pink wisteria shrubs; and an artificial pond with stones placed around it. On the other side were some little trees. Only living plants and the simplest ceramic forms had been used in the design of the gardens. Alice went round to the back of the house, opened the gate and headed towards their special place. There was as much magic in the process of searching for the 'little secret' beneath the wisteria as there had been in its creation. She expected to recognise the withered herbarium from the previous year, to clean the glass and to see, after so long, the flesh of the petals and the bends in the dry stems. But what she found there was an antique Chinese incense vase, turquoise in colour.

Could there have been some mistake?

At the bottom of the vase, Alice discovered a mother-of-pearl casket encrusted with gold and shells. In the casket, just as her aunt had told her, was a key. In fact, there were two: a small, familiar one; and a second, she had never seen before. She made her way out from behind the wisteria, opened the door with the key she had recognised in the secret hiding hole and went quietly up to The Nest, where she searched the shelves, rifled through the cupboards, opened all the flaps and drawers and threw the lacework covers off the table. When there was only one drawer left to open, she found the gilded key was a perfect fit for the lock. It was shaped like a Chamberlain key, clearly marked with the monogram 'M.E.' and an inscription on the reverse: 'WE NEVER DIE'. She felt a chill run down her spine as she reached for the back flap of a watercolour sketch "little trees" on the wall and pulled out strands of hair and some ancient documents. One contained an appeal from the daughter of a conquistador in a manuscript dated 1597 that had been written on her behalf with the aim of certifying the rights of ownership to property that belonged to her. A second document was an original Oztoticpac Lands Map, drawn up to settle a legal dispute over land ownership rights. The black-and-red manuscript showed the locations of fields, houses, palaces, trees, and parcels of land, in the bottom left-hand corner of which were images of garden trees to which European cultures would later be grafted: apples; pears; and pomegranates.

Who is Fitz? she wondered. Beside the documents was a perfume vial from which she pulled a note '*in obi (waist sash) from the kimono that the item is the property of the V& A Museum'*. It was a bilingual counting rhyme, one side of which contained the line 'Lu killed Lo' and the other 'Will Lo kill Lu?'

There were several Chinese ornaments on the ancient vases in the house, along with dinner sets made of Meissen porcelain with its distinctive logo – two crossed swords – and some luxurious Ming Dynasty vases. The secret of Chinese porcelain had long been a mystery in the Western world. Alice knew all about the alchemist Böttger and his numerous attempts to invent it and an exquisite white glaze in Saxony, after his studies of a white clay from the Schnoor estate used in the manufacture of wigs that was similar in content to Chinese kaolin. But why was here, in the place where they kept shared Lady Swan's secret? A pile of advertising leaflets and bills lay in the hall. The envelope on top was a week old, according to the postmark. She found a message among them about collecting a parcel containing some more Meissen porcelain. The note smelled of rosemary. In another envelope marked 'Priority', she discovered a statement from a local bank whose last line referred to a hotel: the Eurostars Porto Douro. She knew one interesting fact about this seaport. Many years ago, the mayor had come up with the idea of introducing steam locomotives to the centre of the medieval city, a project later realised by the French architect Eiffel. Lady Swan had known many things, but, though she and Alice had chatted so much about scientific accomplishments, fairy tales, and the secrets kept by museums, they had never once spoken about love. *Why didn't my aunt ever tell me her personal story?* she wondered.

The first 'Poste Restante' parcel Alice came upon contained Lord Chesterfield's *Letters to My Son* and Philip Zimbardo's *The Lucifer Effect*; the second, *A Book on Tasty and Healthy Food*, published in the USSR in 1969, along with some literature from Harvard University. There was a short treatise about the nature of human pain, revised editions of Salman Rushdie's *The Satanic Verses* and *Midnight's Children*, and a study of India and Pakistan imbued with mysticism and magic. The third parcel held a martial arts monograph, *Taiho Jutsu Kihon Kojo*, describing the fundamentals of a modern hand-to-hand combat system specially created by a group of experts for the Japanese police in 1947, and two Irish histories: Cooney's biography of John Charles McQuaid; and Foster's *Oxford History of Ireland*. The last contained a work on state military theory by Charles Tilly and Dante's *Divine Comedy*. The titles sounded to the young girl like the symphony of an alpine river and Beethoven's 'Ode to Joy', the anthem of the EU, all at once. She felt that she should adopt the same approach to them as to the afterlife of the secrets she had shared with Lady Swan. Her postcards – stuck with stamps like in the old days – and the parcels from Austria had all been kept under safeguard by the house. Not even Nanny knew about them.

'How can I find you?' she asked Lady Swan aloud.

The scent of roses will lead you to the right place, my little bird, the landlady answered in Alice's head.

The Secret Room, London

The General was gazing at *The Morning Walk*, a painting that lent an uplifting sense of contentment to a young couple. Gainsborough's portraits inspired him with their silvery-blue and olive hues and the intimate way in which the artist depicted the aristocrats of a bygone age. The General was recollecting his last conversation with an unknown man in the British Museum. A stirring discovery had recently been made: an X-ray analysis of a picture of the composer Johann Fischer had shown under its upper layer of paint was a portrait of William Shakespeare. Tucked beneath the canvas in the huge wooden frame on the wall of the Secret Room were some interactive maps of New Babylon that helped him to model events in real life. The frame was also the door to the main interface of New Babylon, whose hard drives were concealed behind it.

One day, the Reverend had taken the General up on an invitation to the Secret Room, where he had been troublingly struck by the set-up. Every single detail of the space had been carefully thought through – or rather it was the *absence* of detail that had been masterfully considered. There was nothing in it other than soft lighting and a canvas. All the elements had been tastefully concealed and recessed, except for one: the print from Francisco Goya's *Los Caprichos* on the wall. The General recalled how the Reverend had stoically suppressed any display of emotion until he had taken pity on him and lit up the dark etching inside the gilded frame. On the huge surface of the canvas, pictures in the *capriccio* style had suddenly appeared. Then the General pressed a button on a remote control, and the lighting in the room had changed, creating new spatial images. No trace of the *Capriccio* pictures was anywhere to be seen.

'Illusions, cousin, are just as essential an element of the space around us as reality,' the General declared. When he pressed on the remote control again, a decorative furnishing made of the rarest kind of steel had appeared. It was an enormous desk that looked like a torpedo, whose surface contained a bare minimum of technical elements, screens, gadgets, and other creative resources.

'Very eye-catching!' the Reverend commented.

When the General pressed another button, the space above the desk had come to life. A small terracotta figurine appeared and rotated several times on a podium struck by beams of light before being lifted by invisible jets of air. It was a symbol of a woman from ancient Mesopotamia. 'The basis – and the vulnerability – of the whole system,' the General had let slip, though it was unclear whether he was being ironic. When he switched to different lighting, the figurine vanished as though it had never been there.

As he was leaving, the Reverend had asked the General whether he could recommend a medicine for the bouts of nostalgia to which he was occasionally prone, who had advised him to follow Dominic Harris's advice as he had. The General had always remained true to himself.

The minimalist space in the Secret Room had not undergone any changes before now. This time, when the General pressed a button on the remote control, *The Morning Walk* disappeared. A world of interactive maps opened up before him: their coloured lines, as alive as the channels of rivers and oceans – in perpetual motion, overlapping, merging together and swallowed up by one another – became stiff and stopped moving. Today, these maps looked to the General like the ocean floor. It was as if the body of this flawless security architecture had shifted decisively to a different place.

A newsflash flitted across the top and bottom of the screen: *No active news. Attention. TRANSITION.* According to the prescribed algorithms, the machine would return to active mode after the Transition. The General would not have any hints whatsoever from the machine until the process was complete.

After his former employee Simon's departure ten years ago, the laboratory's staff had been disbanded. The General had exercised his right to be the first person to be kept abreast of the machine's unique recommendations. New Babylon made it possible to model worlds and play out scenarios as to how crises might unfold. The machine would calculate the various ways in which such situations could develop more accurately than the experts and his entourage had predicted on every occasion. New Babylon was equally attentive to tiny details and consistent patterns that might slip by unnoticed. Only the General and his AI knew how many lives on the planet New Babylon had already been saved. However, the price of human life and war scarcely troubled those with whom he was obliged to have dealings – leaving aside the Reverend and the bizarre sermons he regularly gave. The question that therefore now occupied the General's mind was: *What is the connection between world events, the 12th Transition and the Dresses game of Augustin Hoffman?*

He searched the archives to find correlations between the dates on which the Transitions had been launched by the machine and the occurrence of global events. New Babylon's first Transition had coincided with seismic activity in the Indian Ocean and the first democratic presidential election in Ukraine. A second Transition had taken place after the disaster at the

Fukushima nuclear power plant. The third had overlapped with the launch of the social network Instagram, which was no less popular than Twitter or Dresses. However, the recent Transitions of the machine have taken place more frequently. Under the impact of new technologies and the Internet, the real world has changed, and many of the processes in it have been accelerated as the rules of the game in the outside world have become tougher. Robots and programmes had learnt to copy quotations, headlines, and narrative styles to take account of the preferences of a mass audience on social networks; to write little speeches; and, as had now become clear, even compose lines of poetry. The gulf between an original work and its copies had ceased to exist, if one took into account the particular features of the behaviour of a terrorist or blind fanatic. Yet it was only now that New Babylon was turning to a TRANSITION KEEPER for assistance.

Just what was it that had befallen the world this time?

The General brought up the content of the interactive maps on the screen, which lit up a further map of the military flashpoints and conflict zones: 36 wars in 28 countries. New Babylon occasionally issued news summaries that made it possible to keep track of special operations. He had not discovered among the news items any illegal activities of an organised crime network associated with Hoffman.

For the time being, he did not have any answers to his questions. The General pressed a button on the remote control, and the sleeping map once again ceded its place to *The Morning Walk*. He remained in his seat for a few moments, gazing at the smile on the face of the young Miss Stephen, before heading to bed to sleep the sleep of babes.

TRANSITION KEEPER

As she drove to her destination, TRANSITION KEEPER established patterns between all the logical chains, financial tables, alphabets, and formulae, including the formula for the atomic reaction during which the Higgs boson[19] particle was discovered, ending at the speed of cosmic light and becoming one with all the powers of machine intelligence.

The GPS indicated that the car had reached its destination. TRANSITION KEEPER left the vehicle by the sea and headed towards the foot of the sacred hill, the entrance to the Christ Temple in Portugal.

TRANSITION KEEPER felt a shock of pain and lost consciousness. Her physical and aural sensations now existed outside the confines of her physical body and space and time.

---

[19] An elementary particle in the Standard Model of particle physics produced by the quantum excitation of the Higgs field. It was initially discovered at CERN and named after the physicist Peter Higgs, who, with five other scientists, proposed the Higgs mechanism in 1964 to explain why particles have mass. The Higgs boson model subsequently made possible the construction of a quantum field theory.

DAY THREE

Bishopsgate Gardens, London

Richard dropped the General off in the heart of London's business district. The interior of the Ivy City Garden's Gallery restaurant looked far less elitist than The Berkeley as a meeting place for him and the Reverend to drink tea. It was noisy because there were no walls between the kitchen and the dining area, but His Grace was not at all discomfited. He found a spot beside a window looking out over Bishopsgate Gardens from which one could enjoy a good view of the little streams of everyday life as they flowed past.

On spotting the General, the Reverend immediately perked up. 'Why don't we put Wittgenstein's poker[20] to one side today and just have a heart-to-heart? Will you join me in trying the chocolate torte? The one they make here is as good as any you'll find in Europe's Michelin-starred restaurants, he enthused.

The General nodded as he sat down. 'Thank you, Reverend, but I still haven't developed a sweet tooth.'

'It would be helpful to hear what your young gentleman has to say about it. Didn't he claim that the disruption of the presentation had to do with divine Providence – that Hoffman had put the soul of the devil into the machine?'

'Giovanni has not yet returned to Old Chiswick. He merely

---

[20] A heated dispute between two prominent philosophers, Karl Popper and Ludwig Wittgenstein, which took place on 25th October 1946 in Cambridge, England.

wrote to say that the presentation at the Blue Lagoon had been hit by a few technical glitches. He asked for a little money as a loan and has gone on leave.' The Reverend began to feel uncomfortable. He thought highly of Giovanni. Besides being a babysitter for his pets, his cleaner, and his gardener, he also played an important role as a teller of stories about his son. His Grace preferred to say nothing about this last role, however, and quickly turned to a new topic of conversation. 'General, have you heard the news? Yesterday, there was a miracle at Toledo Cathedral. One of the cardinal's hats turned to ashes.'

'I simply adore episcopal legends. You can rest assured everything is under control in the world.' The General was recalling the behaviour of 'El Transparente' – the architect Narciso Tomé and a pupil of the great sculptor Churriguera – who invariably prompted fury and admiration in equal measure, sowed 'horror among academics and amazement among the people' and with calculated bravery once punched out an aperture in an arch through which light fell into the cathedral and emblazoned the walls. He had combined art and sculpture in such a way that no other work would elicit so much controversy and polemic. The cardinal's hat, meanwhile, hung by a single red thread. Legend had it that, should it fall, his soul would ascend to heaven.

It started to rain in Bishopsgate Gardens. A smile flitted across the Reverend's face. While gazing at the bright, drifting, ill-defined faces of the visitors reflected in the dark ceiling of the Gallery of Angels, he remembered the only woman he had been with recently. One of those bright stains reminded him of her pleasing face. When the stain on the ceiling disappeared, the Reverend recalled her question: *Isn't love more important?*

The rain stopped. A peaceful humidity filled the square, and passers-by folded up their umbrellas. The Reverend tore himself away from the view outside the window. *So the cause doesn't have anything to do with the woman?* he pondered. The changes in the weather and the contented expression on the Reverend's face persuaded the General once and for all not to reveal to the Reverend that TRANSITION KEEPER, the subject who had replaced the machine during the Transition, was a woman and not a man. He and the Reverend had harboured very different views on the subject of womankind ever since their childhood, in whom the Reverend saw more of the diabolical than the angelic.

The General shook the Reverend's hand. 'Why don't you stop by my place sometime soon? I'll show you what New Babylon looks like. The other day, I procured from Germany a one-of-a-kind replica of an interactive map of the medieval world created on thirty sheets of parchment. A huge number of events are depicted on it, to such an extent that it can be seen as the story of mankind. The map was crowned with the head of Christ. Its world, created on animal skins, is a circle. Whoever drew it understood that the earth was round, even though the Europeans didn't yet know that Africa and Asia existed. The original version of the map was destroyed by the Allies' bombs in 1943, but happily, some colour replicas had been created so that this copy could be made.'

'How fascinating! I shall definitely look in,' the Reverend promised. As he walked away from the walls of the Ivy City Garden, he had no inkling that the General might stay behind to recall the same woman as the Reverend. Her name was Margaret.

EARLIER – MARGARET

Margaret was not like the women the General usually found enchanting. There was nothing over the top about her, yet at the same time, he found her peculiarly enthralling. She was no taller than Isabella I of Castile or Thais of Athens, just as tender and very shapely. While she stood with her back to him, the General scrutinised every part of her from the elongated phalanges of her toes up to her earlobes. He was more interested in her inward-facing curves than her lack of hair. Having studied her closely cropped scalp and slender, feminine forehead with its deep, blueish cavity on the bank of the lake among some huge boulders, the General suddenly recalled a story about American trackers in the days of the Vietnam War.

She turned around and gave him a mocking look, keeping her eyes fixed on him. Her gaze went deep inside him and immediately established an affinity between him and her knowledge of classical art history. She had got under his skin and made his heart beat faster. No, she was no naïve simpleton like Ippolita Maria Sforza. Nor did she resemble the anorexic model Karen Elson, to whom the British designer Alexander McQueen had lent such sophistication with his hats of chiffon and feathers.

'Please call me General,' he insisted.

'Greetings, General. I study the language of rocks. There are many on the shore in the camp,' she disclosed.

'It's nice to see you. You and I have a common subject for some idle chit-chat.'

Back when he was on UN business, the General had acquired a lot of new admirers in political and diplomatic circles in the countries of the Maghreb and the Middle East. Simon had suggested to the General that they get to know the owner of the camp on the shore of the legendary mountain lake of Issyk-Kul in Kyrgyzstan, a professional doctor who was studying Post-Traumatic Stress Disorder. The subject of his investigations was the difficult conditions experienced by people who had been through wars and crises.

'Let's fly over to the camp and go bathing in Issyk-Kul's crystal waters. Alongside traditional therapeutic treatments, its owner uses Eastern practices that are not recognised by modern science.'

'The modern theory of torsion fields? Who is this adept at promoting Eastern techniques in the Western world?'

'Everyone calls him the Bodhidharma. He resembles the patriarch who christened the "Chinese Anthony". He collaborates with military ministries and private foundations. The General smiled. 'How familiar this seems! I remember they would sometimes let private individuals stay on-site. I propose we take half a day's relaxation there.'

When they arrived, the General revelled in the clean air and the sight of the lake's crystalline surface into which flowed an abundance of mountain rivers.

'She looks like a foreign woman and a doctor's assistant,' Simon declared, indicating an individual walking ahead of them along a path between some boulders who was heading for a swim.

'I'd like to take a stroll to the lake.'

'I'll leave you alone.'

'Is it true you are the person who has a passion for smart

machines?' Margaret asked the General as they were walking together. He had probably never met anyone with this character type. The melodic nature of her English pronunciation confirmed what Simon had said about the British origins of this young representative of the female sex.

'You are not far from the truth. I am interested in alternative approaches to crisis analysis and conflict warnings. Tell me, what do they say about me at the camp?'

'They talk less about you than about your machine that maintains the world's security. They say it predicted the end of the age of translators. Thanks to the Internet, translations can be done more quickly and with greater quality, and for that reason, the teaching of languages in schools will soon be replaced with courses on Asian history.'

The look that the General now gave her was one of great curiosity. 'You have your own view on a smart machine?'

She thought for a brief moment, *If that is the best your machine can do when it comes to making predictions, you are trying to achieve something that belongs to the realm of memories, General. It is hardly likely one can understand human nature that way. With the help of your machine, you are only establishing something that is the outcome of mathematical algorithms. In that sense, you have come to the right place – the Bodhidharma has obtained impressive results when it comes to curing those who thirst for miracles. But this does not give my scientific ideas any hope whatsoever. What are you thinking of right now, General – about how you might touch me? That means your machine is streets ahead of you in its computing capabilities. However, it cannot answer the questions asked of it about humankind. Its responses depend on how you taught it to identify the source: how it can work out to what an impulse belongs – man or machine. How do you find out that it's effective, this machine you're so in love with? Every day it opens up the possibility of perceiving eternity. Grasping a living picture of nature at the level of human impulses is easy, but when engaging in mass-scale computing it is important to understand which sources of data you and your machine...*

What impudence! he thought. *Cut from the same cloth as that redhead Simon!* 'You know, Margaret, the machine's analysis of big data includes a multitude of indicators: medical and emotional indices for anxiety levels, particularly in crisis situations. The computing portion may very soon be replaced by nano-technologies. As for 3D models of the component parts of a living organism, that is a very promising topic, but personally, I would like to go back to the problem of the source and differentiating between a vast number of copies. How are you going to understand this problem? What would you, Margaret Evans, a mere mortal, choose?'

A thought flashed through his mind: 'Understand the source! I am starting to get the impression that you, like me, do not believe in anything – or only in a calculation that has angelic power.'

'The nature of actions is many times more complicated and dangerous than that,' she continued. 'You know how to understand the human spirit, General. But does your machine? We have arrived, General.'

She smiled and the military man, already advanced in years, saw standing before him the embodiment of the famous 'Smiling Madonna and Child' at Toledo Cathedral. He could not forget the expression of the acclaimed 14th-century marble sculpture of the Virgen Blanca beside the high altar. Margaret had disappeared. Meanwhile, the camp owner was already hurrying towards him and the rematerialised Simon, dressed in his elegant orange uniform, his arms opened wide to embrace them.

'I'm delighted to welcome you to this holy place,' he greeted them.

The General and Simon's stay at the camp was eventful, and Simon was the first to ask the camp owner about his English assistant when they came to leave.

'Margaret?' the Bodhidharma queried. 'She's not here. She lives a short distance away at a former rehabilitation base for cosmonauts – a one-hour drive. Today's her day off.'

Simon gave the camp that was now shrouded in the shadow of the mountains a farewell glance. Just as on the morning they arrived, it was marked with signs of the presence of people. He noted a solitary, expressive stain, an alien impurity, on the body of this white landscape beside the lake. The stain was actually a gigantic SUV, exclusively released during the post-war period for conducting military operations in deserts.

'You're lucky to have such high-calibre employees,' the General remarked.

'I hardly imagine the Bodhidharma is going to be driving around the vicinity of Issyk-Kul in that tank,' Simon reasoned.

'It's the Millers' security car,' the Bodhidharma confirmed.

'Do you mean Bill Miller?' Simon asked.

'The very same. His daughter is undergoing a course of rehabilitation at my camp. Margaret is teaching her poetry, classical and modern, at the request of her parents. Come! I'll take you to the helipad.'

One year after their return from the trip to Lake Issyk-Kul, Simon took the trouble to find a recent edition of a specialist journal and brought it to the General's office.

'Do you remember Miss Evans?

'Women write articles like this due to a lack of sexual imagination or love. I am most grateful to you for having left us to have a one-to-one talk on the shore of Issyk-Kul. She is a very atypical creature.'

Simon concluded that the General was conducting an investigation of his own into this 'atypical creature'. However, he did not invite him to take a seat across from him as usual. He was also deliberately cold.

'Sorry Simon, I'm busy.'

Simon tried not to let it show that he had an undeclared interest in the events that had been taking place in Margaret's and the General's personal lives. 'She is fascinated by sound frequencies. Allow me to share something a little more interesting with you. Were you aware that she has a son? He looks like Bobby Fischer; he's a splendid little fellow. The boy is studying at college. When he graduates, I intend to help get him a place at the United States Naval Academy.'

'The old military programme with dolphins is going to be shut down soon. Did you know that Margaret is flying to London tomorrow?'

Simon mustered the most indifferent tone he could manage. 'That's good to hear. How is she nowadays?' In all this time he had only been able to find out one bit of news about Margaret Evans: Cirque du Soleil had been willing to pay her whatever she wanted for a show featuring the dolphins she had trained, but she had declined their offer.

'You can talk to her yourself if you fancy doing so. I asked her what she wanted to see. What do you think her response was? "The monument to the animals that died in the war." Can you imagine that? There was also a phrase she let slip at the memorial.

She said, "They had no choice".'

Simon smiled. 'Perhaps someone ought to show her the other London beyond the confines of the great names and rocks. The Aston Martin showroom is only a few minutes' walk from here.'

'Margaret can buy herself an Aston Martin if she so wishes. I will have no objection if you entertain her tomorrow afternoon,' the General abruptly concluded.

If that is the case, a turning point in my relationship with her has been reached, Simon thought. Inwardly, he assessed his chances as being roughly on par with the General's and once again felt a needling pain. The reason why the General was backing Margaret would turn out to be far more elevated than a mere love story or yet another secret nursed by the money classes.

There was a rare glimpse of sunshine in the cloudy afternoon sky above London that 29th February. It was no coincidence that Margaret was returning to London for the first time in many years. The peal of all twelve of the bells of St Mary-le-Bow Church, the famous Bow Bells, could be heard. Since Simon had found out about what happened to his uncle, he had commenced his own story with a clean slate. He did not really believe there was a female on the planet who was worth making sacrifices for because, so he imagined, he preferred to have his own space and not bind his personal life to one woman. He was content with a room at a guest house, a glass of fine wine, and the possibility of sharing his bed with a pretty airhead no more than once a week. In fact, he was lonely – an ungrounded romantic rather than a confirmed bachelor – and had only not met his true beloved. Needless to say, the last thing he wanted was for the woman who might change his way of thinking to be Miss Evans.

But this was precisely how he was now starting to see Margaret. In the flesh, Simon could not tear his eyes away from her.

To himself, he referred to her, in accordance with *Ikigai* philosophy,[21] as the *kodawari*: a 'living embodiment of intelligence, harmony, and energy'. Her manners and smile vaguely reminded him of her namesake, the youthful Queen Margaret. *I was wrong*, he thought. *It wasn't to prove Shannon's theorem of electromagnetic relay that she flew from Britain to the US.* Who could have imagined that the path to Margaret Evans' heart would be paved with relationships with two high-flying cousins, one a dyed-in-the-wool Calvinist and the other the most brilliant mind of the age who had come to believe in the power of his passion for a machine?

She had changed greatly in the few months since they had last fleetingly seen one another at Issyk-Kul. The very first moments of their conversation would have struck anyone by their frankness and intensity. The main thing that he noticed straightaway was her hair, which she had allowed to grow long and was now crimped to her scalp with a bone comb that resembled a crescent moon.

'How long will you be in London?' he ventured.

'Just one day. I have another flight early tomorrow morning relating to an unusual assignment.' She smiled. 'I'm glad you've agreed to join me at the concert at Westminster Abbey this evening.'

---

[21] A Japanese concept meaning 'a reason for being' and referring to a direction or purpose that makes one's life worthwhile, towards which an individual takes spontaneous and willing action. According to the concept of *kodawari*, the first of the five basic precepts of Ikigai philosophy is 'to start small' without justifying any efforts by reference to a large-scale goal.

An understanding was instantly reached between them whereby the thing that mattered most should not be uttered out loud.

'Today is my unofficial birthday,' Simon told her. 'To be born on February 29th in our neck of the woods was considered a sign that you weren't going to be happy. Probably out of superstition, my uncle put a different date on the birth certificate.'

'In Scotland and Ireland, there are different rules altogether.' She smiled again. 'Women are officially allowed to ask men to marry them, and then the men aren't allowed to say no. But I'm not going to make a proposal to you today. I will wait for the next leap year.'

'What have you managed to see so far?' Simon asked.

'The General and I looked in on Saint Mary-le-Bow Church and admired the stained-glass windows.'

'Did you like the church? The bells of Saint Mary-le-Bow were the most oft-cited bells in the folklore of the City of London for hundreds of years. If you were born within their earshot, it meant you were a true Londoner. They rang during the Great Fire of London and again three hundred years later when the church was rebuilt, together with the stained glass in the western, northern, and central windows. Do you know the poet, George Herbert? *A man that looks on glass, On it, may stay his eye; Or if he pleaseth, through it pass, And then the heav'n espy.* We still have a little time. Let's take a walk-through Lambeth beside Waterloo Bridge and wander over to Marble Arch.'

On the way, Simon only had time to pose one question and work out whether he had overstepped the mark in his relations with Margaret.

'Are you leaving the military base in San Diego to take part in the US?'

She looked down. 'I was born at Birr Castle where the LOFAR[22] project is based, as was my son.' She stopped and looked at him attentively. 'So, the General told you?'

They had reached the corner opposite Hyde Park Corner where Marble Arch stood. Margaret looked up, admiring the great edifice sculpted by John Nash. 'It reminds me of Wellington Arch. A Roman quadriga with four horses and a young chariot driver, with the Goddess of Peace rising above it, the prototype for which was Beatrice Stuart. No one knows who the prototype for the young charioteer was.'

They set off towards Westminster Abbey.

'It may interest you to know that I'm planning to complete my scientific activity and return to London very soon,' she said, interrupting his silent thoughts about her. 'Tending shrubs deep in the English countryside is not for me.'

'I hold out no hope you will keep me company as I sail around the waterways that cut across England in an old barge. No white doves will alight on our picket fence of a morning. You turned down the General's proposal that you join a research centre in Cambridge looking into ways of changing the climate by creating advanced technologies. I understand the idea of "greening" the ocean appeals to you more.'

'The General entrusted me with a serious mission. Bringing the child home wasn't worth getting agitated about. Let's go, Simon, or else we'll be late for the concert.'

At the corner of two of the Royal Parks, Hyde Park and St James's, Simon decided once and for all to reject any claim upon

---

[22] A large radio telescope network that makes observations in the 10-240 MHz frequency range. At the time of writing, LOFAR was the world's most sensitive radio telescope before the launch of SKA (the Square Kilometre Array), an intergovernmental radio telescope that will have a total collecting area of approximately one square kilometre.

Margaret's body and bring his questioning to an end. It was hardly likely he could help her any further now in any event. The General knew how to use his connections in high places as a substitute for high passion. Compared to that, what could he offer? A trip to New Bond Street once a year to look at the new jewellery collections in the windows? A visit to his bijou apartment in a converted roof space with a view of Westminster Cathedral's bell tower? *Neither money, love, nor truth*, he thought.

As soon as the concert in Westminster Abbey was over, Richard arrived in the black cab to collect her. As it pulled away from the kerb, she turned and spotted a lonely figure against the backdrop of the darkening sky. She raised her hand to wave, aware that there was only a slim chance he would see her gesture of farewell. It started raining. As the first few drops fell on the convex spine of the car, Simon found himself repeating lines by John Newton, an English sailor in the Royal Navy who captained several slave ships:

I am not what I ought to be, I am not what I want to be, and I am not what I hope to be in another world, but by the grace of God, I am what I am.

That evening, Simon opted not to go to the fundraising evening. Instead, he altered his usual routine and set off for the nearest bar. In the past, he had been equally fond of old establishments like The Shakespeare, infused with the acidic aroma of cheap cooking and ancient times, and hipster hangouts that quickly filled up with a young crowd from all corners of the world, all of whom enjoyed thinking of themselves as Londoners. He had an unwritten rule: he drank no more than three beers at any one venue, during which time he would wait for an attractive girl to show up. In his conversations with those around him, he also complied with the British social convention never to discuss religion or politics. This particular evening, however, nobody appealing appeared, and after his third drink he headed off to bed. He awoke the next morning to the chirruping of birds in Vincent Park. In the sky above Westminster Cathedral's tower with its 'Edward' bell, he saw a huge rainbow, remembered the previous evening and began counting down the days until Margaret's return to London.

As it turned out, however, he did not visit the bar for a week until he discovered that Margaret Evans had not returned. In fact, she had vanished. None of her telephone numbers were still active; her email addresses were no longer in any databases; and her bank cards, insurance policy, and health insurance in the United States had been cancelled. She had apparently disappeared off the face of the earth.

She conducted a thorough analysis of a database of computer clouds and servers. The database resembled an invisible neural network that was constantly being supplemented with new subjects, playmates, and transactions. She studied the players' rankings and their financial transactions. All the playmates had the same motivation and were eager to win. The rules of the game had remained unchanged. Millions of transactions between playmates were awaiting the authentication of the Black Cloud.

She no longer felt pain. The level of cytokines in her body increased rapidly.

When she opened her eyes, she realised what was at the top of the Holy Mount where the Sacred Heart of Jesus Sanctuary was located.

'Give me water.'

'You were talking in your sleep, quoting strange texts in an *ancient dialect.'*

There was no need for Tomaso Poggio's instant image recognition programme. She came to her senses, opened her eyes and saw a man in her hotel room whom she immediately recognised. Water returned her strength.

This was Celtic.

'Chinese Anthony, how much time has passed?'

'Half a day. Are you familiar with Halton's hypothesis?'

'Not entirely.'

'The abbot of the Basilica came over here to listen to them. He told me that the people in the cathedral believe you are Saint Lucia. The interpretations of her writings hinted that she would return or else we face complete destruction. She did not give any reasons. They have been awaiting her return to the temple for more than twenty years. I don't mind keeping you company in your role as a saint.'

'I am not Lucia Santos. Now everything boils down to one servers address.' A souvenir pen turned into a palm-leaf quill in her hand. 'This is of the Black Cloud. The site of the "ontological gulf and Pain". I know why we met at the foot of the Holy Mount.'

'Are you sure it's worth anything? It is nothing more than an address on the Internet.' The Chinese Anthony sounded a little disappointed.

'Leave me alone for a few moments to get dressed, then I'll show you my car that will take you to the meeting place. Let's go and deliver this message to the General. You have a long journey ahead of you.'

'Forgive me! What should I say to the abbot?'

'That I'll pay him a visit next time.'

'Individual abilities will be expressed through some sort of word or symbol. The more important this characteristic, the more likely it is that it will be expressed through the sign of the ouroboros. A circle held in an embrace by tongues of flame, for example, might symbolise material savings. Tell me about her, the woman from the Dungan race who came to you at the camp.'

The Chinese Anthony looked at TRANSITION KEEPER in surprise. 'Lu? I have no news from her. She visited the camp many years ago, just like you. '

At that moment, they heard a child's voice calling out to them inside.

'Lucia Santos! We've been expecting you.'

TRANSITION KEEPER handed him the electronic key to the car. 'Press the cruise control pedal, and the car will work out the route on its own. Deliver the message to the General's man. In the meantime, I'm going to make a few technical calculations. I need to compare and contrast yesterday's meteorological data, the extent to which the water in the lake heated up, and the intensity of the impact of solar flares on the earth's magnetic field. There are no correlations between them that have led to changes in my state of health.'

DAY FOUR

Porto, Northern Portugal

A huge dragonfly disappeared into the clear sky of the city. Alice disembarked at the Campanhã railway station. With her from Austria, she brought only a small luggage with a boa and a Lady Swann brooch and walked down Rua da Estação to the Confeitaria Sical, where a moustachioed waiter was skilfully wielding trays and cups of coffee. She tried the signature dish, a Portuguese pie whose secret recipe was known only to a handful of local monks. Then she set off down the tiny, steep streets alongside churches dressed like brides and adorned with *azulejo* tilework, admiring the façades of handsome houses embellished with French windows with wooden shutters and wrought-iron balconies until she reached Praça da Liberdade. A little to one side was Mount Oval, home to the city's Jewish community since 1380.

The city's noisy lower district, Ribeira, had a special austere charm all of its own. Most of the buildings on its shore dated from the age of medieval conquest. The square was surrounded by commercial alleyways that led down to the river. On the opposite side, the northern bank of the River Douro was dotted with the best port bars and rowing clubs. The river plain was also known for its orchards and vineyards, whose young white wine was considered the most popular vintage in Portugal. Alice skirted the embankment to the hotel, passing three bridges – the Maria Pia, the Arrábida, and the Dom Luís. The stone building of the Eurostars Porto Douro was concealed within the cliff that propped up the upper town. Towering over the cliff was the convent of the Franciscan Order of St Clarissa.

At the hotel reception was a man who resembled a chaplain and wore the dark beard of a conquistador. A golden badge shaped like a little key adorned the lapel of his jacket. He immediately noticed Alice's hair with its dyed-green ends.

'Welcome, little lady! You look just like the infant Mary, the first Duchess of Porto, the Austrian Maria Leopoldina! A room has been booked for you on the first floor. It has a splendid view of the river. Alfonso! Room thirty-three!'

The porter popped out from behind the door. He was a teenager, the same age as Alice. *His hair was clean and glossy – like the infants painted by the artists of the Spanish Royal Court*, she thought.

'Allow me to show you to your room. Are you from Belem?'

'Not quite. I'm from Innsbruck, the city with the Golden Roof. Have you heard of it? Maximilian the First wanted to make Innsbruck a golden city. There are palaces there where beautiful waltzes are held. I could invite you to a Viennese ball if you promise not to step on my toes.'

Unfortunately, it looked to Alice as though Alfonso— optimistically named by his parents after Alfonso I, Regent—did not know how to dance the waltz. Alice enjoyed teasing him a little, though he didn't know whether she was laughing at him till he turned and gave her a fiery look.

'Listening to you, I thought you might be the Alfonso who founded Portugal against his mother's wishes,' she baited him.

'I am descended from the last Knight Templar who defended the gates of Tamar Castle.'

'The twelfth century William of Tyre?' Alice loved Templar stories. In books by William F. Mann that Lady Swan had sent her, she had read about the spiritual order of the Knights Templar and the feats of Hugues de Payens, who had participated in the Crusades that took place in modern-day Israel, Syria, and Europe. In the recesses of her memory, she recalled her final words: *You know what to do should you ever be in danger. You know where my house is and where the key is.* Once something had captured Alice's interest, it never needed saying a second time.

Alfonso stopped in front of the door of Room 33. 'I'm no lord of the manor, lady. There were a lot of children in my family.'

Alice stopped behind him, looking pleased. 'Well then, you must know all about the local cuisine? I bet you love fried chestnuts and *rodízio*.'

'You're not like all the other girls. Most of them go surfing or gawp at the local tourist attractions. But you didn't come here to look at the churches in Lisbon.'

'So you work as a guide too?'

Alfonso opened the door with an electronic key card. 'Your room.'

The French windows looked out over a landscape of former military warehouses and monasteries on the opposite bank of the Douro. Alice entered with a majestic gait while Alfonso loitered at the entrance. Something told him that she did not want him to leave but nor did she want to let it seem as though she found his company interesting. She turned to face him.

'How do you like it, Alfonso, a descendant of Gottfried de Saint-Omer, André de Montbard, Hundomar, Godfron, Roral, Joffroi Betol, Nivar de Mondesir, and Arsambo de San-Anyan? This is for you – for your efforts and interesting conversation.'

He did not take the tip she was offering and took a step backwards. Alice let out a sad sigh as he shut the door behind him. Suddenly, her daydreams were interrupted by a furtive knock. She felt a visceral fear, as though she were in the presence of some primal threat.

'May I, sweetie?' came a voice from behind the door.

Into the room came a young man with chameleon-like, jet-black eyes. Alice watched him from her cramped hiding place in the wardrobe. With a notepad and the Meander in one hand, he opened a box of pies, closed the shutters on the French windows and moved towards the chestnut desk. With the other hand, he pulled out a notepad and pressed on the cover of the Meander. Seagulls shot up into the sky and started squawking. Swans and ugly ducklings. Breathless giant turtles. Silvery deep-water fish with birthmarks. A deer taking flight over the horizon. Stony-faced mountains. The first ray of sunshine on the tarmacked road leading to the swimming pool.

Alice let out a loud sneeze, and their eyes met as her head tentatively emerged.

'We meet at last, little sweetie. Oh, how I adore pranks and chicancry! Why were you hiding from me?' He wanted to tear off her boa with a brooch.

'I am not afraid of you, Salazar.'

A sudden gust of wind blew both of the French windows open as the chaplain appeared at the door of Room 33.

'Let the girl go at once! Little lady, how can I help you?'

'I didn't mean her any harm,' the young man protested. 'I just wanted to play with her.'

When the chaplain joined arms with those present, Alice suddenly turned pale and became incredibly beautiful. Her cheeks turned a rosy hue as she saw a gigantic illusion with womanly traits rising over the Douro and the Monastery of Serra do Pilar as though they had been transported to the time of Lucia

Santos.

'The Eighth Coming of the Blessed Virgin Mary,' she whispered.

The room began to fill up with poplar catkins that had flown through the sky from the banks of Cais da Ribeira. The fluff cascading in through the windows hung in the air. The embankment was covered with a mass of flowers. Jubilant shouting and prayers could be heard amid the roar of the crowd. Reporters and onlookers were running along the street. The chameleon with drooping shoulders dropped to his knees and began muttering. The notepad fell from his hand to the floor.

'Oh God, I am a beast! The desire of all pitiful beasts is to live without pain and suffering. I have seen many like me who have wasted their miserable lives for the sake of money and fame. They trembled for their miserly pleasures; they grasped at them. I didn't want to be or become one of them, but I have never known anything else.'

Reaching down to the floor, Alice picked up the notepad with the Meander on it and handed it to the chaplain, in whose hands she saw an octagonal chest adorned with gemstones. The layout of the stones reminded him of a political manifesto. The chaplain knew what to do. He took the astonished girl into the adjacent room and through an emergency exit into the internal courtyard, where a dark green car from the local taxi company awaited them. Then he opened up the notepad and examined it carefully. There were no lists of contacts or clues at all. The light on the Meander went out. The chaplain handed the chest to the driver.

'The little lady's nanny will be waiting for her next to the Basilica of Bom Jesus,' the driver told him. 'The word on the street is she's the daughter of Saint Lucia.'

'We can do without your gossiping! Did you see the Marian apparition in Porto? It's all everyone's talking about here.'

Meanwhile, the man who looked like the chaplain returned to Room 33, took off his false beard and glanced out of the hotel window at the embankment. His real name was Taylor.

EARLIER – TAYLOR

Taylor – or 'the chaplain' – had begun by mixing paints in artists' studios, whose canvasses over time began to build entire states of being. He had also managed to acquire a number of remarkably rare paintings at auction and provide tip-offs about some of the biggest scams of the century. The unofficial information he had obtained proved to be valuable and accurate. He changed his name when he began to get involved in protecting artworks and unique *objects de beauté*. This only partially explained the nature of his mastery, however. He had a huge number of nicknames – one of which was so long that no one could remember how to pronounce it – and would present himself as a descendant of a Portuguese king who had disappeared in the 14th century. Ten years before, when he and the General had met at a Maison Assouline party, he had introduced himself as Taylor.

The General had proposed he get involved in a task associated not with protecting artworks but a living and breathing human being – with whom, as he saw it, a machine might not be able to cope. Taylor thought the project sounded interesting. Over time, the General became convinced that he was unrivalled when it came to deciphering technical codes and putting his knowledge into practice. Taylor did not use a phone but could be found at the British Museum. The previous year, he had asked him to organise the little girl's trip to Austria and her meeting with a certain lady.

Montcalm Royal London House Hotel, London

There were several viewing platforms in London that afforded breath taking panoramic vistas of the roofs of the buildings and allowed one to observe how the city had slowly changed over time. The Victorian rooftops had gradually merged with the architectural lines and post-war construction from the previous century, adorned with upper terraces with plants and picnic tables, which had in turn given way to islands of gleaming skyscrapers that depicted the modern face of the metropolis. Within their brazen splendour, they hid the labyrinthine 'crossings' to buildings on the lower level, where ancient religious objects fought for space with relics, gates, cathedrals, and ritual structures in the foundations of office blocks.

The doorman at the entrance to the Montcalm Royal London House Hotel opened the door with a welcoming smile as the General's black cab came to a stop in Finsbury Square in the City of London. The General walked up to the upper terrace that afforded one of the best views of the business district, where he found Simon in the company of some unknown Greek god.

'Have you heard the news? They're saying that Hoffman has vanished,' the General began breathlessly.

It was as if those ten long years of oblivion and silence had never happened. He found to his surprise he was pleased by Simon's re-invasion of his life. Talking to him once again gave him an injection of strength just as it had in the past.

'Don't you find this remarkable?' Simon pondered. 'In the last twenty-four hours, there has also been a rapid rise in the number of people complaining about having their Internet shut off and in calls to Lost Property departments. There is one rather odd thing. Not a single technical malfunction was recorded anywhere on the planet. If you want my opinion, the balance of the world has not changed over the course of a single day. In places not affected by conflict, people are constantly losing their lives due to acts of terrorism. But today not a single person has died.'

'Stranger things have happened in the world. What would it take to surprise me? If there were no traffic jams on the roads and all the trains ran on time! I was speaking to a Nobel laureate from Heidelberg University and to Paul Nurse,[23] the chancellor of Bristol University, one of the UK's redbrick institutions. No one there knows about Hoffman's innovations, but they have heard about a young scientist, destined to have a great career in the US and the UK, who worked on developing a nano-microcarrier of certain brain flows based on the Human Brain Project.[24] The formula for a nano-booster of the brain was one an acquaintance of his, a neurophysiologist, had come up with. Inventions like this could be used to cure large numbers of people of illnesses and for other purposes. Who knows how far he might take his exclusivity!'

---

[23] An English geneticist was awarded the 2001 Nobel Prize in Physiology or Medicine for the discovery of protein molecules that control the division of cells in the cell cycle.

[24] A scientific research project in the fields of neuroscience, computing, and brain-related medicine. Initiated in 2013 in Geneva, the HBP is largely funded by the European Union. Its primary objective is to create an ICT-based joint information and research infrastructure.

'I checked a story about an event that occurred: the blowing-up of a car containing a well-known journalist in the in Ukraine. The crime remained unsolved; none of the extremist groups claimed responsibility.'

'In the outside world, thousands of unforeseen events took place during a Transition, each of which was capable of causing a butterfly effect composed of the reactions and actions of individual people, radical groups, and criminal gangs: conflicts; crises; disasters; weddings. Could the death of one journalist be considered as grounds for the proliferation of an undetected threat?'

'I found out something else for you, General. A message was sent this morning to Hoffman's phone from Austria: "I have found your Schrödinger's Cat[25] – TRANSITION KEEPER". And a photo of a map with a location: a house in Austria.' Simon showed him a mugshot on the screen. 'Asian woman with the stamp of superiority on her face who drowned this morning.' The General gazed at the image, intrigued. If one ignores her Asian ethnicity, the woman in the photo looks like Melania Trump. The photo had been taken by Irving Penn, who in the course of a creative career had composed a multitude of beautiful and stylistically varied pictures for *Vogue* magazine as part of a series called 'American Beauty'. *She is indeed very beautiful,* thought the General.

'This is not TRANSITION KEEPER?'

'The young woman's name cropped up in some police

---

[25] A thought experiment, sometimes described as a paradox, devised by the Austrian physicist Erwin Schrödinger. The scenario presents a hypothetical cat that may be simultaneously alive and dead, a state known as a quantum superposition as a result of its being linked to a random subatomic event that may or may not occur.

reports from a small resort town beside a lake that stated she had committed no law-and-order violation nor breached the borders of the United States of America.'

'You were right, General. The virtual voice banner at the Blue Lagoon was *her* voice. It is most likely that she is the author of the message.'

'You probably still have some friends in Newbury.' The General was surprised by the speed at which Simon had worked.

'Her name is Lu. So, she was in Iceland the day before the trip to Austria?'

'I suggest you find out what the local police chief who investigated the case thinks about all this. Do you want me to get in touch with him?'

'Are you inviting me to join you in looking for TRANSITION KEEPER? I would be delighted.'

The's mobile phone let out a plaintive sniffle as a handsome young man with sensitive features appeared on its screen. The Simon had pulled some strings to get him to call. 'Have a word with him – be tougher with him,' he whispered.

'I am the General's personal assistant. Now, why don't you tell us what happened yesterday?' Simon asked, switching seamlessly into German – another of his talents that the General had loved to observe in the past.

'The body hasn't been found yet,' the caller replied. 'She came here to attend a golf tournament on the crest of an alpine ridge. We spent the whole day playing in the fresh air. She had a fantastic drive and an ouroboros tattoo on her shoulder. 'I know what life is like in little villages. It is in precisely such places that the most horrifying events often take place. You believe in miracles – I can recommend a great priest for you too. But I can't guarantee that your secret will remain a secret unless you tell us honestly what happened. When did you realise she was no ordinary tourist? What did the two of you talk about while you were together?' Simon was playing the inquisitor brilliantly and gave him no let-up.

'About life at that foreign woman's guest house. It was a big place, but she didn't try to make a single cent out of it. That's all I know about her.'

The General and Simon exchanged glances.

'Have you met the landlady of the Austrian house on any previous occasion?'

'No. The landlady pays her taxes promptly. Believe me, I will be very, very happy to help you in any way I can. You can trust me.'

'Each of us pays every time. Only the price is different,' the General declared as they parted company. 'The local police chief is certainly not up to scratch for the role of Nietzsche. There's something that doesn't ring true about the story. The woman starts by bringing the local police chief some joy and then takes an interest in the landlady of a local guest house. Then she sends that message and disappears, leaving her clothes behind as though she wants people to think she's dead. For a woman with an excellent golf drive, she's not as straightforward as you might think. And one thing's for sure – she didn't travel deep into the Austrian countryside just for a few rounds of golf and a bit of hanky-panky with a married cop!'

'How did Lu Salome know about TRANSITION KEEPER's existence?'

'The fifteenth stone... that's the main tourist attraction in the city of Kyoto. Do you know about the garden of Ryōan-ji?'

'No. I've never been to Kyoto.'

'Picture it – a rock garden made up of fifteen untreated black boulders spread across the garden's white gravel. From whichever angle visitors look at the garden, they will only ever be able to see fourteen stones at a time. The fifteenth always remains outside their field of view, screened by its neighbours. If you take a step across the wooden gallery that extends along the edge of the rectangle of sand – on the other sides, the garden is hemmed in by the stone walls of a monastery – once again, you see only fourteen stones.'

Simon imagined the space in Kyoto that the General had described. One step, two steps, and then a third step. Galleries were built and recreated without people noticing. And then, amid the brilliantly designed chaos, a new composition comes into view in which one of the stones disappears.

'Forgive me, Simon, I'm wanted elsewhere, but thank you for taking part in the investigation. I must admit, you were pretty good at questioning the squire.'

The General exited the white stone terrace of the hotel, leaving Simon alone inside the membrane of the glass bubble in the company of the nameless god. When the waiter brought him the bill, he knew what to do. He would set off for the Austrian countryside to find out just what kind of game Lu Salome had got embroiled in and to seek out the fifteenth stone in the Ryōan-ji Temple Rock Garden.

TRANSITION KEEPER

TRANSITION KEEPER *copied the signal from the Meander and hurtled upwards, above the power of the black, luminous images created on the surface of the earth by the hand of the god Ra. Above Picasso's bulls. Above Saturn's rings. Above the dark piles of clouds, like the neck of a dragon, beyond solar systems and galaxies, beyond cosmic black holes. And even higher than the mathematical rows of the Black Cloud. She could distinguish between multiple flows of physical and biochemical reactions related both to deep animal instincts and the greatest human accomplishments as she continued to glide across the surface while adding to their ranks, delving into an abyss of the primitive states of being of living things – contentment; aggression; enjoyment; pain – measured by the size of values and the ratios between nuclear reactions that lie beyond the subjective bottom of cell division. TRANSITION KEEPER could recognise and foresee the reactions of vital entities regardless of their form or habitat. All dissolved like the DNA of a multitude of multitudes.*

The Meander's coordinates matched those of the subject's previous locations for the unveiling of the new set of the game in the Black Cloud. TRANSITION KEEPER *identified a number of playmates with the track of the game and locations, changed the status code of the subjects she identified with reference to all the video and audio data, and sent warning messages to police departments at all the airports.*

EARLIER – NEW BABYLON

The first supercomputer Transition coincided with the tragic events of 9/11 and had flagged up for the General and his team the problem of terrorism, which could not be solved by AI since it required additional studies of such concepts as love, sex, faith, and death. It had initially collected and analysed data about the flow of money around the world. When the programme was launched, however, New Babylon had insufficient knowledge to identify threats associated with the data value 'human error'.

After the first Transition, New Babylon began collecting and analysing data from museums and libraries, learning new tasks and discovering recurring events throughout the history of humanity in every field from astrology to astrophysics.

After the second Transition, it added data from commercial networks and shops to its updated version, along with popular resorts, clothing brands, and trashy novels.

After the third Transition, New Babylon began to use a language made up of symbols to process lists and to identify and distinguish between different manifestations of how people behave in areas of military conflict and when they are living in peace.

After the fourth Transition, it added face recognition to the program.

After the fifth Transition, it integrated weather forecasts and predictions of other energy flows in the biosphere.

After the sixth Transition, linguistic research, including

gengo saikatzu, enabling it to analyse the structure, musicality, melody, and phonetics of speech, was added.

After the seventh Transition, New Babylon had learned how to analyse large data flows, circumventing the traditional mass media systems as it did so. By then, mobile devices had become a feature of the modern world.

After the eighth Transition, the program incorporated into its operations a set of algorithms for analysing large quantities of data about the millions of people using social networks.

After the ninth Transition, it began accurately predicting the precise time at which new revolutions, military conflicts, and political tensions would arise and also discovered the reasons for many of the worst man-made disasters and accidents all over the world. The superintelligence displayed remarkable abilities when it came to identifying events that had not yet been conceived or manifested, which became unique tools for warning about all manner of threats. It had continued to solve tasks that involved a high degree of danger. The information that the General obtained concerned every one of the strategic analytical and decision-making centres, as well as financial and military institutions.

In the aftermath of the role played by New Babylon in the Arab Spring, interest in its activity had increased, and the General signed a number of major government contracts in the United States and his first big contract in the Middle East. All the while, he was monitoring conflicts around the world, including the war in Syria and events in Libya, Yemen, and Nigeria. After the most recent Transitions and the perfecting of the versions of the program, the machine had learned not only to decode values but also to foresee with great accuracy the 'chains' of real events taking place in the world. The General was always among the first to find out the results of elections and test cases, along with people working in the media. When New Babylon itself predicted the unexpected coming to power of several political figures, a host of respected experts acknowledged that it was one of the few machines that were genuinely capable of self-development.

The General is now set about creating the Secret Room in the trendy borough of Battersea. The glory days of New Babylon's rising star had begun.

DAY FIVE

The Secret Room, London

The General was delighted when a call came in from Simon. He had begun to get back into the rhythm of their chats from all those years ago and had vividly imagined how today's conversation would begin. 'The fifth day of the Transition is usually particularly important. Have you read the news yet? It is starting to look as though a global truce has come about climate change in Austria.'

'But how long will it last?' Richard appeared. 'An unusual incident took place in Malaysia yesterday: two computers began talking in an unknown language. A number of servers in the States were blocked because the conversation between the two machines caused a massive system overload. Now there's little chance of us finding out what they wanted to talk about! And this morning, the eighth Marian apparition occurred in Portugal. I would like to have a look at the aerial photos taken from above the Douro.'

'I don't have them yet, but they'll soon appear online and in the mass media.'

'The process of interference with a positive sign may have been brought about by TRANSITION KEEPER in the event of a threatening programme.'

'Have the photos of the apparition above the Douro been forwarded to us yet?' the General queried.

Richard nodded. 'The window showing a weather intelligence company's forecasts for notable events did not indicate any such physical phenomena occurred between two and six a.m. That's all the official announcement said. No pictures have appeared anywhere in the media yet.' He handed him a piece of paper. When the General unfolded it, he found all it contained was the address of a small joint-stock company.

'Who delivered this message?'

'It's a message from TRANSITION KEEPER delivered by the Chinese Anthony. He came over here in a beautiful car Tatra 77. It was manufactured in 1933. Only two hundred and forty-nine of them were ever made, plus four prototypes. From the southern bank of the Thames, there has been a request to let you know that warnings have been received by the police units at all the airports. Do you want to talk to them?'

'No. Right now I need to verify this information.' Be guessed the General's mute question and added. 'There was not a cloud over England.' New Babylon restored the image with light and mirrors, adding some volume and crisp lines. 'He held out the drawing.' Richard nodded.

TRANSITION KEEPER's vital balance was reset to zero. It happened then in Portugal, at the moment of Lu's annihilation in Austria.

New Babylon was blinking away merrily on the wall with news updates.

Reykjavik, Iceland

Fitz – aka Peter Schutz – was speeding towards Reykjavik under cover of rain and seven rainbows. He recalled the stories Simon had told him about the city, what an unusual place it was and how it was no accident that Hoffman had chosen to hold his presentation there. He hadn't noticed anything unusual. Nor was he inclined to think that a peace treaty between the United States and Russia that was signed there, marking the end of the Cold War after so many years, could have been Hoffman's reason for choosing the location. The observatory had been built on the site of a former British airport, whose spherical shell attracted one like a magnet. He took a quick look at the extinguished dome on the hill and recalled something he had heard a former naval officer say, who was now working as a scientific adviser to the US Defence Ministry: *Plashes of sunlight are the part of the stream that took a different route.* He remembered the story about how Bobby Fischer, the brilliant chess player who had attempted to rewrite the rules of the sport, had once visited Iceland.

On reaching Reykjavik, Fitz decided to go to Old Havana on foot to revel in a state of being to which he was unaccustomed: that of an ordinary traveller. His route through the Northern Shore took him via the parish church of Hallgrímskirkja and the enormous open-air concert hall and museum Harpa Reykjavik, whose surrealist mosaics reflected the sunlight like the colour of the high sky, tinged with violet. In Old Havana, a different kind of evening atmosphere prevailed, where trawlers wove among the piers accompanied by flocks of hungry, screeching seagulls hoping to grab some of the catch for themselves. *There must be some other link in the chain,* he thought. Fitz took out the Montblanc pen he had pinched from Hoffman and examined it, unscrewing the cap and taking out the ink cartridge. It was just an ordinary writing pen, he realised, feeling a trifle disappointed. You surely couldn't use it to turn off the power and disrupt a presentation.

He sat down at a restaurant table. The place was typical of Havana and served traditional continental cuisine. Once he had sent the transcript of the interview to Simon, he began scanning the headlines from a sheaf of fresh newspapers taken from a shelf by the hearth.

THE LAST DOLPHIN. IS IT REAL OR JUST A CLONE?

Why was he here? To see with his own eyes the real landscapes that were later reworked into the marvellous virtual world of *Game of Thrones* or to read advertisements? He turned the page.

HOW CAN YOU ESCAPE LONELINESS?

THE MOST BEAUTIFUL ROUTE ON THE ISLAND. STUNNING PANORAMAS. A BLACK BEACH

Stopping at the last headline and putting the local press to one side, he decided he had already had his fill of the landscapes of the Northern Shore outside the window. He set off along the most beautiful route in the south-east towards Reynisfjara and its unusual beach of black sand. He was simply trying to count the time since Margaret Evans had left him. That night on the island, he would dream of dolphins. They were using their acoustic 'melon' lenses to make beckoning sounds, which were not being bounced back to them via an echo as was normally their way.

The next morning at the reception of the Icelandair Hotel where he was staying, Fitz was informed that a table had been reserved for him in Fischer's restaurant. He was overjoyed. Fitz and Simon had spent much of their spare time together surfing on all the world's continents and oceans. A while later, they added more activities, like mountain climbing and diving. 'You have to train the body, not spoil it,' Simon had always said, who also loved to quote the Russian general Suvorov: 'Train hard, fight easy!' Fitz had tried to share with him his passion for studying. Then, when the time came for the strategy of those training sessions to be replaced with a strategy for fighting, he had fully committed himself to this new activity and discipline. Desires flowed through them easily; they did not seek pleasure and profit.

As Fitz left his hotel room opposite the observatory, the gulls of Old Havana seemed quieter. He walked into the restaurant, sat at a table and asked a waiter to bring him the day's papers. Scanning the headlines, he alighted on one of them:

BERLIN ARTIST RECREATES THE FEATURES OF THE VIRGIN MARY

He looked closely at the photo under the headline. It couldn't be! 'Are you Fitz?' asked a woman behind him, holding out her hand to him in a business-like fashion. 'I'm Liz.'

He leapt to his feet like a little boy. 'Nice to meet you, Liz. What can I treat you to? A glass of chilled wine?'

'I doubt a glass of white wine here will be a treat. I'm used to fine wines. The same goes for the company I like to keep.'

'We crossed paths at "the edge of the earth," do you remember?'

'I had time to call in at the Blue Lagoon to find out more details about the events. I was told that the unveiling of the

Perfect Nanny didn't take place due to technical reasons. Some of the corporation's staff confirmed that the professor has gone on holiday.' She sat down opposite him. 'I'm also told you might be able to help with the investigation into the high-profile murder of one of my fellow journalists. Fitz is the old French word for son. I wanted you to know. Our organisation trusts Simon.'

Twilight was descending over Old Havana. The other diners at the restaurant probably assumed they were a couple. A waiter came over, lit some decorative candles on the table and set down two glasses of wine and a little dish of raisins.

'To you, Liz!'

'I need evidence that might shed light on the tragic circumstances of the death of a specific person and the car bomb. How are you going to help with the investigation into such a high-profile matter, Fitz?'

'I don't conduct private investigations in places where military conflicts are taking place. I'm a journalist for a US scientific publication who ended up at the presentation with some others. We are talking about a different degree of conflict relating to future threats. A variety of threats may be involved. It wasn't in a painting that I saw that animal.'

'I got the impression it might have been his competitors who disrupted the unveiling of the Perfect Nanny. Forgive me, awkward oversights are completely normal in my line of work.'

Fitz felt a little stinging sensation in the part of his body in contact with his chest pocket, from which he pulled a gold-tipped pen and handed it to her. 'I took this from Hoffman's desk. It's a remote control; it also emits a signal. Imagine if the signal were to be strengthened!'

His mother had promised to get him a pen like this as a gift the last time he saw her. She had had a difficult relationship with

God, creating and destroying things with ease, and Fitz had had a difficult one with her. He still could not admit to himself that he loved her. *No news from her for ten years*, he thought.

As he pressed the golden cap and turned his gaze towards the depths of the restaurant, his eyes met those of a ghost. Its figure in silhouette was clearly copied from the portrait by the Berlin-based artist he had read about in the local press who had painted the Marian apparition in Portugal. The phantom muttered something and then vanished.

Two text messages arrived on Liz's phone, which she busily set about reading. 'I need to go back urgently to check something. Let's talk again tomorrow. Same place!'

As she got up from the table in a hurry, Fitz turned to look at the lounge by the fireplace again but this time saw nothing there. *I must have imagined it*, he thought.

When the owner, Fischer, opened the door, Liz almost crashed into an extremely tall, well-built man. The notepad with the Meander on it had been left behind on the table, whose cover Fitz noticed was blinking anxiously. Pulsing through his consciousness was a sentence about pain from the end of the interview with Hoffman. Meanwhile, the burly man had come up behind him and was trying to strangle him. The smell of fish made him feel nauseous. Pain shot through his chest as his mouth and nose filled up with blood. Fitz caught sight of the now strangely twisted ghost, which this time was opening its mouth silently as though emitting an invisible wave, like a dolphin cast onto a deserted shore. He breathed out forcefully and hit his adversary in the groin. When he finally knocked out the foul-smelling man, the ghost disappeared, and Fitz and Liz dashed out of the restaurant in the blink of an eye.

Melting away into the twilight, they moved quickly, cutting

corners along the narrow alleyways of the port as they approached the Icelandair Hotel. Within a quarter of an hour, they had reached it. Festive and noisy, the guests were enjoying the evening by drinking cocktails and warming themselves beside the hearth. In the bar, there was baseball on the TV, and music was playing. Fitz felt a sharp pain in his jugular vein. Judging by the way the receptionist looked at him, word had already got out in the city about the spot of bother earlier.

'The General will be pleased to see you,' he confirmed. 'Here is the number of the helicopter and a permit to fly for two people.'

He held out his hand to her. 'Liz, let's fly away from here together.'

'I'm sorry, I can't. I need to do my duty. I promised you an exclusive if the facts were confirmed, and now I've received official information.'

They stepped out into the night and walked towards the heliport. For a moment, she stopped to admire the clear black skyscape embellished with the dancing green ribbons of the Northern Lights. 'Wouldn't you like to live here, house number five, on the edge of the earth?' he ventured.

'No, I wouldn't,' she smiled. 'Sleeping in the last room in an outhouse, even in a respectable old castle, is not for me. I will be your ghost, Fitz.'

My mother used to speak like that too, Fitz thought, recalling the features of the spectre who had warned him about the danger. 'So I wasn't imagining it after all,' he murmured.

The Secret Room, London

The emergency channel interrupted their exchange of views. A face appeared on the monitor by the door to the Secret Room, opening its mouth like a live fish thrown into a hot pan. It was the Reverend.

'I'm sorry, Richard – it appears we have an intruder,' the General apologised as he admitted his visitor.' Find me everything about the event in Ireland. Contact Rekjavik.

'Give me a clue!'

The General playfully replaced the painting in the massive frame on the wall of the Secret Room, and Gainsborough's *The Morning Walk* gave way to William Hogarth's *Marriage A-la-Mode*, whose graphic art was filled with piercing irony and hidden details. Anticipating the chain of events that would result from the Reverend's appearance in the Secret Room, he had gone up to his office in advance to meet him.

'Next time, please make sure you warn me you are coming, cousin!'

'Is that some kind of joke, General?'

'Not a bit of it, Reverend.'

The General pressed a button on the remote control, and his office chair turned into a Danish throne adorned with the horn of a unicorn and silver lion guards. On seeing this, His Grace became even more enraged.

'Is the Danish throne not to your liking?' the General enquired. 'For many years now, I have made allowances for you.

If only that unauthorised Marian apparition in Portugal hadn't happened!'

'I have no doubt you and your machine intelligence were directly involved! Ten to one the Pope, the Patriarch of Constantinople, and pretty well all twelve of the Imams will be demanding an audience with me. What would you have me do?'

The General maintained a friendly tone to attempt to calm his cousin down. 'Marian apparitions have occurred many times around the world at Lourdes, Ruda, and Guadalupe. Why all the fuss? As though this were the first time! Talk to them! For people who don't have enough knowledge about matters of faith, one could construct a wonderful sermon out of that alone, let alone the subject of a new ghost of the Holy Mother.'

'I have a new parish, cousin – God and ordinary people who have no one to look out for them. Surely you do not suppose that your god with a female face is pointing out to mankind the path to light? What's the point of all these experiments anyway?'

'You are clearly overestimating my abilities, Your Grace. I would be glad to be the original cause of events that could have engendered the best sermons ever heard, but alas, neither I nor my machine meddle in the events of history.'

When the Reverend's gaze fell on Hogarth's painting on the wall of the Secret Room, he turned crimson. 'Next time, please replace the Hogarth with Goya's *Deceit and Greed* or *Of what ill will he die?* In the meantime, are you hinting at my servant?'

'I'm not hinting at anyone, Reverend. I simply wish to understand what has made you so agitated. Please take a seat! Some floral gin from the Botanic Gardens? To the pleasant outcome of an extraordinary phenomenon!' When His Grace declined the offer of an undiluted glass, however, the General realised that quieting his power-seeking relative would not be as easy as he had thought.

'You didn't say a word to me about the fact that your machine had handed over control of global security to a woman. That is your responsibility. You also kept me in the dark about the most important thing of all: Will God now have a female countenance? I am officially declaring my opposition to your superintelligence, General. You're striving to effect a situation in which experiments are placed above the Church.'

'I sometimes get the feeling you keep a revolver concealed beneath that cassock. Let's stop talking about opposition in this traumatic world of half-truths!'

'Who is this female your machine endowed with the rights of God? I mean, what kind of woman is she? White? Chinese? African-American? Mexican, Armenian, Jewish? Or perhaps she is transgender? After all, trans people are entitled to love in this world too, are they not?' The Reverend felt tired from all he had seen and needed to rest.

For the first time in all their conversations, the floral gin and the changing of the paintings on the digital screens had been of no use. The General resorted to his final argument without holding out much hope of a favourable response. He carefully switched on some additional lighting, and a sculpture of the woman from Mesopotamia appeared and began rotating in the air in front of them.

'If only I knew, Your Grace.'

'If you don't stop this, the Church will never see eye to eye with you, General!'

Together they watched the sculpture of the woman hanging in the air, which had been a gift from Simon. When the General switched off the light, it disappeared.

'I don't think I've ever told you about my secret terrarium

cage, Reverend. It contains only female specimens. Would you like me to show you something you've never seen before?'

The Reverend sat motionless in the Danish prince's armchair. 'Goodness, I see. So you've been studying the issue of female aggression? You put them all together in the same place. But tell me, how on earth do they reproduce?'

'Don't gripe, Reverend! Who other than me would you expect to know all of your peccadilloes? You would never let a woman get anywhere near you or large numbers.' The General pressed a button on the remote, and one of the walls of the Secret Room turned into part of a different space about which the Reverend had not the slightest inkling.

'What do you need that cage for?'

The General ignored the question as one of the Secret Room's walls was transformed into an arc made of green wood with cream-coloured flowers like the Spenser Pavilion. Through it, the Reverend could only see one face of the environment in which the animals lived. In the distance, he made out the gleaming sphere of the Bird Dome.

'Females never come back,' he growled.

Both animals and plants were in the tablespace. Mosses appeared on its threshold, and a flickering light played on the surface of the water. Further off, the voices of birds and animals' mating calls could be heard. Meanwhile, from the direction of the Dome, a snow-white platform, adorned with a stone Golestan Palace or Palace of Roses and embellished with marble, mirrors, paintings, frescoes, tiles, and wood carvings portraying magical beings, began moving towards them until an Iranian throne appeared in the Secret Room. Finally giving in, His Grace stepped forward as his rage was dissipated by his favourite tipple.

The General waited for the gin to work its magic as the

question at the centre of their discussion was temporarily forgotten. The wooden shutters—or their virtual imitations—moved aside to let the platform into the terrarium cage as far as the Gates, where he encountered a huge sacred fig tree.

'I hope a little stroll won't be too tiring for you. I assure you, Reverend, you won't get bored. The park was developed by the architects who worked on the "Gardens by the Bay" in Singapore. You are now beside the Tree of Wishes. Make a wish!'

'You have taken many of my wishes into account, General, but your temptations are not for me. Neither Jesus nor the Buddha nor Mohammed nor you yourself, the God-and-Father, have convinced me, you see.'

The Reverend moved across the platform above a cascade of artificial pools decorated with little bridges, where gigantic reptiles came occasionally into view. The General was waiting for this journey to capture the Reverend's imagination completely, at which point he would pause it. Having remained behind at his desk in the middle of the Secret Room, however, he continued for now to lead the excursion.

The platform arrived at an unusual structure whose dome resembled an observatory with two magnificent pavilions: the Dome of Flowers; and the Rainforest. It was the crowning glory of this creation by the Singaporean architects, landscape designers, and experts in the fields of biology, mineralogy, and botany who had come together as one. As it slowly opened, thousands of tiny coloured birds darted out of it into the artificial sky, forming a living picture of the vibrations and sounds of an unrepeatable beauty and mathematical harmony. The Reverend gave the impression he liked this special visitor attraction. The expression on his face noticeably brightened, and his cheeks bloomed with a rosy hue. He was experiencing long-forgotten feelings of inspiration.

'Shall I ask the birds to put on a concert for us?'

'No, don't!'

The Bird Dome closed itself up again, and each of its inhabitants perched obediently on a branch.

'I'd rather you explained to me what she is, General. Some latter-day Mother Teresa or Indira Gandhi? What help can your TRANSITION KEEPER, on which New Babylon has bestowed its attention, possibly be in our world of falsehood and destitution? Or was it just that you didn't have any better ideas up your sleeve? If she is a virgin, General, your mystical story cannot have a close relationship to the truth. I have no conflict on matters of faith. Jesus came to us in a male body. I don't understand why New Babylon didn't choose someone of the male gender as its *locum tenens*.'

'You insist that the body is taboo, and yet, as you say, Jesus appeared as a man. I have no objection, but nothing is certain. Stop reducing everything to the level of a brand identity, Reverend! We must thank nature – she houses more of God's creatures too, apart from those that are evil spirits. Would you like to take a look at my praying mantises?'

'Count me out of your executions!'

'I have some extremely curious specimens and whole organisations to study. Look at these delightful creatures!'

An enormous, pyramid-shaped ant farm rose in front of the Reverend, who watched for a while the life going on inside it.

'So you mean to say that a biological organism of the female sex temporarily receives the machine's skills, retaining her human traits all the while and in all likelihood points to the true path? Allow me to ask you one question: Has she had children?'

'Listen, Reverend, maybe that's what I would have wanted – for a famous actress or singer to be in TRANSITION KEEPER's place, or some animal no one has ever seen before. If that were the case, it would be far easier to explain to the clergy and congregation what has occurred. But what has happened has happened. New Babylon has protected its personal information in any event. Don't forget that knowledge is my domain, cousin! If the latest scientific discoveries are to be believed, animals are far more advanced than man. Did you know, for instance, that they pass on memories, whereas we hide them from one another?'

Knots of muscle flickered across the Reverend's face. The General could see every change in the picture clearly.

'How long has it been since your last underwater journey? Look up!'

The Reverend threw his head back. A fish tank shaped like a huge soap bubble was suspended in the terrarium's artificial sky over his head. An enormous plaice reclining on a chessboard could be seen through the glass and appeared to be changing colour to imitate its squares.

'Don't you fancy trying out the Sicilian defence?' the General's voice rang out gleefully.

'No, I don't want to play! Not after hearing your stories about how artificial intelligence has become the greatest chess master in the world, a champion at Go and Shogi, and has created a "children's machine"!'

'Or else tomorrow our own offspring will start conducting experiments on you?'

'Ah, how marvellous! There are dolphins in your terrarium! Now that's *far* more interesting!' exclaimed the Reverend, suddenly distracted.

'Why exactly does that surprise you?'

'They're a rare species.'

'I collect rare species. Look towards the horizon!'

For the sake of such a spectacle, the Reverend climbed down from the platform and hurried on before pausing to gaze at some vertical crystals.

'Those are the chromosomes of the animals,' the General explained. 'It is time to come back now.'

The Reverend shot a farewell glance at the endangered dolphins and clambered back onto the platform to begin the return journey. The ebony partition of the terrarium behind him became invisible and was filled with a silver colour.

The General replenished their glasses with some more floral gin. 'I have told you many times, Reverend, that the living being TRANSITION KEEPER is a transcendental thing, merely a value that is helping to shed light on those matters with which my machine cannot yet cope. Nothing more than that.'

His Grace left in a hurry.

The General decided not to pass on the latest news to Simon. Let him busy himself seeking out the fifteenth Ryōan-ji stone in the backwaters of Austria!

EARLIER – FITZ

Simon had found out about Miss Evans' existence after his appearance at the Reverend's house as an honorary visitor to the Gallery of Angels, which incorporated 3D mosaics of canvasses by the Great Masters and state-of-the-art technical equipment to recreate scenes from the Gospels. Music from a cutting-edge sound system played an important role in the overall effect. According to the official record, she had been born to a Protestant father, Allister Evans, and a Catholic mother, Nora Coren. The couple had failed to secure the blessing of their devout parents for the betrothal and had moved to England to get married. They had both died fairly young, whereupon the young girl had returned to the country of her birth to study at Trinity College in the Irish capital. According to the unofficial version, however, she was brought up at Birr Castle by her adoptive parents. Simon was also the first to have come to know about 'Stendhal Syndrome' while visiting the Gallery. The Reverend had asked the developers to move the paintings to the top so those visiting the temple had to tilt their heads up towards the ceiling for a long time to look at them. He had asked the Reverend why there was no picture of the Virgin Mary.

On leaving the villa, however, he discovered a different answer to his question. On the hilt of a woman's revolver, embellishing a panel of light-blue enamel, was the profile of a young woman with a distinctive aquiline nose and the initials 'M.E.' in curly writing around her. Simon had concluded on the basis of this decorative female piece that the owner of the Temple of Dogs had some personal secrets of his own. His investigation soon led him to a group photo taken at Trinity that included a young priest and a girl. They were both smiling and very presentable. The picture had been taken before they had gone off on a 'mission' with the Red Cross in a country where a brutal civil and religious war had been raging for several years. Simon used the photo to look into the person and background of this mysterious woman.

Little by little, he found out more details about her. The young priest had turned out to be a fervent follower of Calvin and the ideas of the Second Coming of the man-God. However, Margaret apparently preferred to study her Cambridge textbooks on social sciences, politics, and rhetoric rather than recite prayers every day and read about salvation and the Bible, which very quickly gave rise to disagreements between them. At this point in his research, Simon realised that Miss Evans' mission had coincided in time with the great public outcry in Ireland about sexual harassment in the Catholic Church. In any event, it seemed likely that she did not realise she was pregnant when she returned home.

Their story would have been a typical one had it not been for Fitz, whom Simon also found out about after discovering the names of Margaret and her son on the passenger manifest for a flight from Shannon to JFK in New York City. As a result, after their meeting on 29th February, Simon spent several weeks waiting for news until the General announced in a call that he would not be returning to London any time soon.

'Do you want to ask me about Margaret? I do not know where she is,' the General admitted.

Simon then set off to look for fundamental evidence for her

existence. Without saying a word to the General, in the space of a day and a half he crossed the ocean and part of North America. When his plane landed, he immediately turned his attention to his search. To start with, however, he was impatient to meet her son, the young Bobby Fischer, and decided to begin at the college where he had been studying.

When he arrived, the corridors were deserted. Staff in the administrative office said it was the holidays but confirmed that he had spent a year there and shown an average level of ability. In the boy's personal file, Simon saw a photograph of him for the first time. His recorded name was Fitz. Even in his modest picture, he looked like a kid in a promotional ad campaign, blue-eyed and blonde. Simon saw no resemblance to Fischer; if anything, the boy took after his mother. In fact, he looked more like the singer Bryan Adams at the time of his first song, 'Heaven'. During his studies, he had apparently shown himself to be a friendly and companionable young man who had made a name for himself by organising a show on graduation night. Other than that, however, the college's administrators had nothing else that might be of help.

As Simon was leaving the office block, the janitor called out to him and offered his assistance, having heard what he had been asking about. The world was full of people with a desire to make a quick buck.

'Do you know where he is now?' Simon asked.

'Yes. He went on a surfing trip to northern California with his classmates.'

The janitor could not exactly be described as attractive. The only aspect of his outward appearance that people had ever admired was his almond-shaped eyes, which were now a calm, dark hue. They were as capable of calmly and judiciously seducing and deceiving a person as entangling them in a noose of sensuality. On account of this trait, he had been nicknamed 'Regenbogen' when he was a child. The unusual sobriquet had stuck and become his calling card. Simon asked him what he wanted.

'Only money.'

As it turned out, this Regenbogen happened to be a talented raconteur. *Stories like this usually set off the imagination, but they don't have that effect on me,* Simon thought as he listened. When the janitor's portrait of the young man was over, he asked him, if should he see him, to let him know a certain someone wanted to talk to him and that it was about his mother. Then he paid him for his story and agreed to meet him again that same evening.

When the time came, he was surprised to see Fitz at Regenbogen's side. The picture was gradually becoming clear.

'The General came to see me after she disappeared. He made me a present of a Hamilton watch and Mother's pen and handed over some things from her laboratory in San Diego. There could be a great deal to learn from those items,' Fitz reported.

'Is that all he said? Could I have a look?'

'They both said little. My mother, like him, didn't tell me very much. She revealed almost nothing about her work at the military base. That was what you wanted to know about, right?'

'There are rumours about you in the local students' league. They say you can control big fish,' Simon flattered him.

'Is that why you've been looking for me? So, my mother was right when she said I shouldn't demonstrate my knowledge of the divine frequencies to an audience that wasn't ready for it! It made me angry with her at the time. After my party trick at the prom, she and I even had a little falling out before I left.' He pulled a folder out of his rucksack and handed it to Simon. 'In case you're interested.'

There was one miserly note in it about a programme[26] for studying sea mammals and deep-water fish. In the 1970s, a study of dolphins aimed at the discovery of a new language had been conducted at Point Mugu in San Diego. Several teams of aquatic mammals were formed, one of which specialised in searching for survivors of accidents and another for sunken objects, while three were trained to search for mines. They were known as Special Forces and were used during the wars in the Persian Gulf and Iraq. According to American sources, their numbers increased at a testing site on the island of Key West in Florida, where there had been an exercise using dolphin bombers that were supposed to put mines on the undersides of seafaring vessels, but the dolphins refused outright to recognise the targets. Ultimately, in the weeks that followed, the military had to explain themselves to the yachtsmen who discovered diversion mines on their launches. The dolphins had independently altered the solution.

Simon flicked through the records, which concerned hypotheses about how whales might cope. The latter was absolutely essential in order to prevent changes to the climate that would be catastrophic for nature. The latest report by the International Monetary Fund confirmed Margaret's theory. When it came to saving the planet, every whale was worth thousands of trees. Simon also found several notes about submarine-class machines and deep-water fish. Margaret highlighted risks that might arise in the future stemming from the AI used to control technical equipment. Simon recalled that a

---

[26] The US Navy Marine Mammal Program (NMMP), is a programme administered by the US Navy that studies the military use of marine mammals.

report had recently emerged about the invention of a robot submarine called CLAWS that was capable of destroying targets without any interference or control on the part of living beings.

'I didn't have any thoughts about it at all. Before she left, she advised me against starting out on my career with the General,' Fitz summarised.

'His machine has been perfected,' Simon responded.

'I have to hurry to a bachelor party. Let's discuss all this tomorrow.' Fitz was about to leave but turned back.

'Mom was against the idea of putting chips in deep-water fish for the sake of experiments associated with AI. That was the main source of disagreement and the reason they decided to move the project to a different location.'

'Did she leave you alone for long stretches for the sake of her work?'

'She didn't leave me alone. Just the one time, when she went on a trip around Europe with the General. When she came home, she said she had swapped her deep-water research for clouds because when you reach the bottom you can only push yourself off it, but in the clouds, you can drown.'

'What do you think about all this? Don't you want to leave all this scientific claptrap behind you and go surfing on a warm tide somewhere?'

Fitz gave him a studious look. 'Can you surf?'

'You know, a surfer in Nazaré in Portugal rode a wave thirty-two metres high while playing the violin. He's, my idol.'

Fitz smiled. Simon now had confirmation of something he had intuitively sensed: Fitz had inherited more talents from his mother than his biological father. He knew that they would be returning to Ireland together even before the young fellow had agreed to the idea. That evening, Simon decided not to try to justify himself to the General by spouting nonsense about how seeking inspiration in his office job was not in his nature but instead to slip away quietly from the New Babylon laboratory without saying goodbye.

Northern Portugal

The car sped off towards Braga, the ancient capital of Portugal, as Alice started to come round. No sooner had they reached the embankment than she caught sight of Alfonso. He was running as fast as his legs could carry him towards the city centre with nothing on his mind other than his mission to deliver the chaplain's message. Falling like a crow's wing, his black hair fluttered in the wind, and his swarthy skin and movements looked extraordinarily beautiful in silhouette. He resembled the emperor of the Brazilian Empire. Alice shouted out ecstatically as she pointed.

The driver gazed enviously at the girl in the mirror. 'Is he helping you?'

'He helped me take my luggage up to my room.'

'That little bellhop of yours does indeed look a little like Pedro, the enemy of Miguel the Fourth, who asked that his own heart be kept at Lapa Church after his death. Pedro's golden heart adorns the coat of arms to this day. After your meeting with your nanny, I will take you to the father.'

'Did you know my parents?' Alice asked, catching his eye in the mirror.

'I once took them to Granada, to the Hotel Parador. All I know is that they were happy that day. They were a man and woman with great hearts. I don't have anything else to tell you, little lady.'

They drove on in silence for a while as the car climbed ever higher up the hilly, winding road. Finally, they stopped in a square next to the Sanctuary of Bom Jesus do Monte. Nanny hurried over from the door of the Hotel Templo. The driver took her by the elbow, led her a little to one side and engaged her in conversation. They headed towards the hotel opposite the Bom Jesus Basilica so that she was able to enjoy undisturbed a view of 'The Holy Stairway', a staircase to which pilasters were attached and designed to evoke feelings of the boundlessness of the world and the Baroque vagaries of form and shape. It was a chariot flying away into gaping skies. Alice could pick up no more than isolated words from his frank conversation and only heard clearly the last few Spanish sentences.

The driver unrolled a small object. 'The girl's parents presumed you would want to make sure their intentions were sincere.'

Nanny froze, looking more astonished than if she had witnessed the Marian apparition with her own eyes. 'That girl is never going to come back to me, is she?' she murmured.

'I don't know… this was all they asked me to pass on to you.'

'Let me at least gaze upon such beauty! Up until now, I have only heard stories about such a thing. Agate, jacinth, heliotrope, sapphire, and gold with ringlets.'

'The treasures of great dynasties were not created in order to be looked at, you silly woman! Instead of an attic room in Madrid's Chueca district, a bakery in Porto in a nice part of town and generous compensation, as per the contract.'

An enormous dragonfly was flying ahead of Alice as she walked down the road between meadows full of flowers and greenhouses.

DAY SIX

Millstadt See Bay, Austria

Simon got off the first train from Vienna with a crowd of tourists at Spital Millstadt railway station and crossed the adjacent square to reserve a little room at the ERTL Hotel near Millstadt See. The hotel – the oldest in the village – had an unparalleled advantage: from its windows, one could view the magnificent landscape of a ski resort and the snow-capped mountain range that included the Goldeck. The mountain's name translated as 'golden corner' and was the highest point in the region. Simon visited places like this fairly often and had a good knowledge of their inner workings. He found they had a charm all of their own. It was not difficult to pick up what those around you were saying and what was going on. The most trivial event would quickly become known to all, to be discussed over the morning coffee and the shot of schnapps at midday. If one of the locals thought they had solved the first letter of a crossword clue on one side of town, they would go to the other side of town and tell everyone – and nobody, he knew, was more familiar with local news than a hotel employee besides the train station.

He headed downstairs. The only thing open at this time was the family buffet, but despite the early hour, a barman was on duty drying the glassware that was responding with a ringing noise that sounded welcoming. He immediately engaged with his only morning customer.

'I'm Stefan. Where are you from then?'

'London.'

'Want to try my signature cocktail?'

Simon had a conviction that, for any barkeep worth their salt, their signature cocktail should be the one that matched the mood of the customer. 'I'll give it a try,' he chuckled in German, a fairly good grasp of which he had acquired at school.

'Is it the local way of life that interests you or the recent crime here? Did you hear what happened at the lake? Every other customer asks about Millstadt Bay now.'

'Neither, actually. What interests me is the landlady of the guest house at the top of the hill. Her home is known for its two little gardens.'

'So, you want to know about the foreigner?'

'Where does she come from; do you know?'

Stefan respectfully wiped the crumbs from the wooden surfaces in front of him. 'I don't. I haven't seen the person you're asking about, but I know she's managed to turn Austria into Little England in just a few seasons. I've no idea what her real name is. Go and take a look – the tourists who pass by say it looks British. Bit by bit she created two magnificent living gardens around the guest house, and now everyone in this neck of the woods feels duty-bound to grow wisteria and rare Japanese plants. God's smiles can be deceptive. None of the locals have tried to compete with her in the art of breeding birds. She built a swan house on the lake where the birds can shelter from the cold and get fed there too. The folks around here call her Lady Swan. Everyone here admires them.'

'Where I'm from, swans are given special protection by the state. Each one has a ring put on it and is given a number. Such treatment is seen as a right.'

Stefan leaned across the counter to whisper. 'Only the house at the top of the hill doesn't belong to her. This is a very small town, and I happen to know the local notary pretty well. Client privilege on such matters does not extend to conversations between local officials over a glass of schnapps. I can tell you how to get there. It takes half an hour on foot.'

'Does the local police chief here like a glass of schnapps too?'

'He came in to see me a few days ago.' Stefan leaned in again and spoke as though letting him in on a secret.

'He was trembling like a leaf.'

'Why?'

The barman smiled. 'How should I know? It was that same night. All my online social networks went haywire, and my mobile phone messenger stopped working. There was a power cut all over the village.'

'Make me another of your best cocktails!'

Simon thought it would take a while to get over a woman like Lu Salome. From the ERTL Hotel, he made directly for the chalet that had been rented by the now-vanished Lu. When he arrived, it was deserted and enclosed by a police cordon. Some birds were perched on the branches of the trees beside the derelict house that looked as though they were sleeping. *It may be due to the effect of strong electromagnetic waves*, he thought, though the local police were attributing it to solar flares. He descended the craggy hills towards the rear of the house and made his way into the little gardens to take a moment to appreciate their general layout, noticing the blue colour of the Chinese vases. Even by his most conservative estimate, those artefacts sitting unsupervised beneath the wisteria shrubs must have been worth the best part of a million Euros. He found a button inside one of them and a children's counting rhyme written on Chinese paper. *Lu killed Lo. Will Lo kill Lu?* he read.

He took out the contents of the vase and took in the shore of Lake Millstadt, the place of Lu's annihilation. The bay looked deserted. The tourist boat that travelled back and forth between the shores of the lake had not yet arrived. From here there was a splendid view of the opposite shore.

'Are you looking for me?'

A hoarse, powerful voice made him shudder with surprise and spin round. It belonged to a short, sturdy man wearing a dark Sicilian hat. Simon recognised the distinctive features of Bill Miller. The corners of his lips were turned down. He had a tired look on his face, an old-fashioned cigar between his teeth, and a familiar, fiercely metallic gleam in his eyes. He had changed little since the only other time they had seen each other.

'I'm glad to see you again, Bill,' Simon answered him. *What is he doing at the death ground of the woman with an ouroboros on her shoulder?* he wondered. But he preferred to remain silent.

Miller smoked, oblivious to the ash falling on his suit. The expression on his face softened slightly, and his eyes filled with tears as if a song by Sinatra were echoing across the bay. A large blackbird dropped to the surface of the water. Her feathers shone in the water's glare.

'My Sarah is dead,' he said simply. 'She had lost the plot towards the end. Before she fell ill, she went to see shamans, priests, and soothsayers... she was looking for an answer to why Laura had died. I tried to snap her out of it but to no avail. Since you're here, tell me what you've got! What evidence do you have about our Lo?'

The death of the Millers' daughter Laura had gone unsolved for more than ten years. Bill had done everything he could. Hired sleuths all over the place. Set up a telephone hotline. Offered a huge reward for anyone coming forward with information – all in vain! And now there was this note that mentioned her.

EARLIER – MILLER

The story of the Miller family was rooted in the past when Sarah had won Miller's heart through her wealth, beauty, and intelligence. Together, they had created a new legend for New England. The family had pursued some exclusive historical and cultural projects on both coasts of the United States, from New York to California. 'The Miller family is coming tomorrow,' announced the General on the eve of Margaret Evans' arrival in London.

'So, we're dealing with a lucky fellow?' Simon suggested.

'I propose that you too become a shareholder in a new company. New Babylon is not up for sale, as you know full well. The reason I'm doing this is to strengthen my presence in the gaming sector. This market is rapidly becoming more influential right now.'

'Might I be introduced to the family? Many of their friends are potential future US politicians.'

'You're right, Simon. Please attend the event at the NED tomorrow!'

'Take a moment to admire Sarah Miller, General. She is a real Marjorie Merriweather Post.'

The tone of the NED event was set by Sarah. There was a great deal of noisy chatter and merriment around the table. Simon did not find out much that was new from the people he knew there besides the fact that Miller had been backing his wife's ventures. Like her, he enjoyed writing the cheques for the biggest donations. In this way, she had managed to teach her husband the ways of American high society with the help of some astute investments of her parents' commercial capital. Though he was no longer in the first flush of youth, she looked extraordinarily fresh-faced and attractive. Her silky, colourful outfit was complemented by a Cartier Royal collier with Kashmir sapphires and diamonds, and she wore new 'high jewellery' bracelets on her wrists. Simon recognised them as the couple who had never hired jewellery in Manhattan. The Millers had acquired the accoutrements to underline their own enigmatic nature and that of their relationship. *An aristocratic classic never goes out of fashion*, he thought as he gazed at her. *Men like that*, he pondered, *usually choose their partners based on a simpler principle – inheritance* – until she seemed to sense what he was thinking and began staring at him intently. Then she smiled and mouthed *andante, andante*. He recognised the musical term and responded with a respectful nod of the head, but the look he gave her was intercepted by the watchful and suspicious gaze of her husband under his brows, whose expression at that moment reminded him of one of the famous masks at the Cesare Lombroso Museum. As Simon unhurriedly scrutinised the faces of the guests, he wondered why it was that God rewarded seemingly unattractive people with a strong inner desire and, conversely, bestowed an attractive appearance on those who were indisposed to experience either earthly or heavenly love.

An attractive gossip columnist from one of the glossy magazines attempted to engage him in conversation. 'The Millers are at the top of the list of the biggest donors to charitable causes in the United States. I'm not at all surprised that Sarah Miller has returned to London,' she gushed. 'She studied at Cambridge; her family covered the cost of her architecture degree. She wasn't particularly successful academically and was not known for being very industrious, but for all that she still managed to become something of a legend while she was there. In fact, she was the muse at Robinson, one of the university's three women-only colleges. When she returned home, she set up a foundation, raised large amounts of money in donations and made some very generous gifts to her alma mater. Miller has been helping her. The two met at a party at the famous Ansonia House and have been together ever since.'

'They're about to announce the launch of a fund to help pets and immigrants. They won't raise much money here though,' commented an editor from a respected Washington publication as Sarah took off her collier and wrote the first cheque to get the fundraising started. The assembled audience gave her a round of applause. Simon got to his feet.

'It was bold of you to ogle my wife like that over lunch,' Miller told him when they bumped into each other as he was leaving the room. He felt a shiver down his spine like he had as a child when his uncle was explaining to him the rules of survival in a hostile world. Ever since Simon had fled from him, he had adroitly avoided getting into conflicts with that kind of person. When he had no option but to cross paths with them, however, he knew how to behave.

'Forgive me – I didn't mean to offend you. It was the magical effect of the precious stones on your wife's neck. I just wanted to express my admiration. Sarah Miller is a veritable legend in the Wild West and New England. This is a present for your wife from the General.' He handed him a brooch in the shape of a swan with a diamond.

Miller gave it an appraising look. 'How can one know the true value of gems? Precious stones serve eternity, whereas man appears only for an instant.' From the satisfied look on his face, however, he clearly liked the gift. 'So, you are one of the General's men? Will you be at the gala dinner tonight? My wife is very excited about it.'

'Believe me, no one knows how to surprise people quite like the General! A great time will be had by all without my needing to be there.'

The two men bowed politely to one another and parted company. After their first encounter, Simon had not understood what it was that underpinned this mutual attraction between him and the General. Only now, ten years later, did he realise that its basis was the unique and remarkable Sarah Miller and her daughter Laura.

Millstadt See Bay, Austria

Simon felt for the military button in his pocket and the note written on Chinese paper. The next moment, Bill Miller was reading every word of it, pursing his lips as his eyes took on a dry shimmer from the closely interlinked waves. The children's counting rhyme had made an impression on him far more powerful than Simon could have imagined.

'That's my daughter's handwriting. She used to call herself Lo.' He let out a heavy sigh. 'Are you wondering why no one ever suspected Lu?' he asked, as though reading Simon's mind.

'I don't understand anything about Chinese counting rhymes.'

'I shall be with you and in you. I shall love both your darkness and your light.'

'What did it mean by that?'

'I'll be back, no matter what happens' Said Simon

'I trusted her. She promised to tell us who killed Laura. Lu knew people in the Asian cartels. To them she was untouchable. I always expected her to provide the answer to the rhyme right up until the last moment. Then, just before she died, she suddenly made you the executor of her will, Simon. Now I understand why – it was because of that note. Where did you find it? It must have been that clever little so-and-so Evans who gave it to you.'

Coming from Bill Miller's lips, the name of Evans took Simon by surprise, displacing all his other thoughts. He suddenly realised that the investigation into Margaret's 'disappearance' had come to an unexpected denouement. Many a time had it gone that way for Simon in his childhood. It was like developing photos – first, you take the film out of the cassette in a darkroom, next you mix some chemicals, and then you release the paper into a tray of liquid until the image emerges, slowly but surely, like a memory. At his school in Berlin, his physics teacher had led a photography club, and over time he had become a fairly accomplished photographer. That was something else that always surprised him: how much effort was required to make true images come through using old development techniques. Such was the case with the old snapshot of Margaret, whose life had gradually turned into Miller's Holy Grail.

Bill Miller gave a satisfied chuckle. 'So, you didn't know that Margaret Evans remained a hostage in our dispute? Today, thanks to you, my argument with the General has ended in a tie.'

'Were you able to check every person?'

'That wasn't necessary. On the plane with Margaret flew the General's daughter, Alice.'

'And Sara doesn't want that they died.'

'No, I didn't know. So, you knew Lu?'

'Yes, me and Lu were in contact in the States. The General knows all about it.'

'Do you know how she died? Maybe it was premeditated murder.'

'I don't care.' Miller's tone softened. 'I'll keep the note. How much do you want for this scrap of paper?'

'Nothing.'

'No money at all? Why not? Why are you refusing to accept a reward?' Miller was looking at him with suspicion and speaking in a tone that suggested he would brook no argument.

'Now that Sarah is dead, I don't want to talk about her any

more. And remember, no one must discover that my daughter was deliberately killed.'

'No one is going to find out about the note,' Simon assured him. 'Should it occur to anyone to ask why we met here this morning, we were merely discussing house prices in the Bay Area.'

Miller nodded. 'Is there anything else you need from me?'

'You never met a friend of hers by the name of Hoffman, did you?'

He sighed again. 'I can't remember.' He handed Simon a package. 'Take this, it's for you. It's a recording of my daughter's last conversation with Miss Evans. As a token of our gratitude.'

See, Simon would muse on how, in all the time that had elapsed, he had never guessed the truth: the owner of the Austrian guest house and Margaret were one and the same person.

'God's smiles can be deceptive. Knowledge and feelings cannot decide on the punitive measure. But I need to determine the measure and form of the punishment for certain individuals,' he heard a woman's voice say. The voice sounded like Lu Salome's – he imagined it sailing across a body of water until it suffocated from happiness, like a spirit not in the habit of looking at the sky.

The place had begun to fill up with holidaymakers, whose children were staring at the rafts of ducks and wedges of swans. As if by the waving of a magic wand, two enormous grey replicas of Miller emerged from the shadows without disturbing the bay's tranquillity, where the first ferry of the morning had arrived. His bodyguards flanking him, he headed towards the town's main drag that was lined by a fence running alongside some cornfields. Simon watched him go. There had been something he couldn't quite put his finger on in their conversation, as is invariably the way when you touch upon stories that have their roots in an irrevocable, distant past. When the tourist boat had weighed anchor and set sail for the opposite shore of the lake, it seemed to him as though there were two spirits present, one of which was that of Sarah Miller.

Old Chiswick, London

Giovanni was dreaming of the Ferris wheel at the fair in Liverpool, which was spinning backwards – a blessed sign in his system of calculations. For him, the events of the last few days had been interwoven with anticipation of the big moment.

In Iceland, a couple of days ago, he had met the most beautiful woman, who wore a tattoo shaped like a circle of flame on her shoulder. He thought Fortune was capable of smiling more than once and had agreed to her proposition. They had chatted for a while about the General's self-learning machine, after which she handed him a notepad with a Meander on its cover, with whose help he would be able to earn a huge sum of money. Subsequent events had gone well until he had pressed on the Meander in the hotel room in Porto and a ghost had appeared, followed by a chaplain. He had only just managed to escape by pretending to be a religious fanatic and had decided to forget all about the notepad. Then he had gone back to the Reverend, who was waiting for stories about the miracle of Lucia Santos. Needless to say, Giovanni did not disappoint him.

'Your Grace, I witnessed the Marian apparition in northern Portugal. A lush blossom fell from the sky as though it were early spring on Mount Fujiyama. Hundreds of people have started believing in the glory of our Lord.'

'Everyone here has lost interest in that,' the Reverend had said, a note of bitterness in his voice.

When His Grace returned to the Temple of Dogs from the

Secret Room, he had already guessed part of the truth. Giovanni asked him why he seemed troubled.

'There's no particular reason that I can see, my boy. I just feel anxious.'

'I'll call the mini-pig over here – perhaps he'll cheer you up.'

'Not today.'

'Should I turn the music on for you in the gallery?'

'That's not a bad idea, my boy. But first I have a few questions for you...'

'Of course, Your Grace.'

'My son...when was the last time you saw him?'

'The time he and I performed on the same stage at the graduation prom at his West Coast college. There were bagpipes playing in the background.'

'Tell me about him!'

Giovanni was well aware of the value of putting the old man in a wistful mood and knew how to transform his tendency to nostalgia into recollections of pleasure. 'I didn't really know him well. He enjoyed a lot of different things but had no respect for religion, angels, or demons. I never saw him go to church.'

'What sort of things did he like?'

'He was a guy who liked to joke around like everyone else. Played the fool. Sometimes got into fights. On the day of the prom, we had gone out in a little boat to celebrate. I was asked to help. The students were all standing on the port side. He was the only one on the starboard side when someone suddenly pointed out a whale. Then we all heard this really weird sound, like some powerful call, which shattered all the crockery and glassware. Then the whale waggled its tail, pushed an enormous wave into the air and swam off. Nobody was hurt, and afterwards, we all warmed up by drinking spirits out of paper cups and teasing each other. Everyone saw it happen but thought it was just a coincidence and he was only messing around. But it seemed to me as though he had been saying something to the deep-water creature. As for me, I spent the rest of the evening sweeping up glass dust.'

Just like his mother, the Reverend would usually mutter at the end of conversations about his son. 'You're good at reading between the lines. A few hours ago, I saw a dolphin specimen in the General's Zoo. Articles have been written saying that it's extinct. Perhaps there are unknown capabilities hidden in the walls of his room.'

'Did he tell you anything about your son?'

What face does Fortune have? Giovanni wondered as he walked into Chiswick Park across Classic Bridge. A creep of tortoises could be seen on the small islands around the reservoir, whose dark shells looked like wet, black stones in the sun. He turned towards Goose Foot and sat down on a bench with a view of the amphitheatre, obelisk, and Ionic Temple, recalling how the Reverend liked to quote a line of verse by Andrew Motion: *We can look directly at the sun.* The obelisk, the site chosen for the meeting, was a place Giovanni knew well. He admired the play of shadows on the steps of the Temple, enjoying the gleaming sunbeams on the little pond. In summer, he and the Reverend were in the habit of taking leisurely strolls along the pathways and over the picturesque little bridges, accompanied by a multitude of dogs of all varieties tearing around its green spaces. It was with good reason that the locals called the place Dog Park.

A shadow fell across him as he brooded on the park bench. He looked up. A man emerged from the penumbra of the green labyrinth and sat down next to him.

'Nice to meet you. Augustin Hoffman. Have you heard

anything of the General and his new tool TRANSITION KEEPER?'

Giovanni grimaced. 'You have found me at last. So that was what I saw in the hotel room in Porto! She's too young to be a secret weapon!'

'I want to believe you, Giovanni. I was on the embankment in Porto yesterday too, and I saw the results of the interference as clearly as I see you now.'

The face in the sky. I am not interested in the notebook. I want to have you as a main player in my game, Giovanni! I'm going to transfer a sum to you for the new prize fund that will be enough to make all your dreams come true.

Blue Lagun, Iceland

Hoffman was in the Blue Lagoon, sitting in a Marc Newson Lockheed Lounge reclining chair, dressed in a trendy patterned shirt and boots. He cast an eye over the unassuming suit and military bearing of the final representative of the press on the list. 'You have fifteen minutes, tops,' he warned him politely.

The editor from Henry Stewart Publications, a publisher of science journals, used the opening lines of the press release as his starting point. 'So, the Dresses app is a thing of the past. You have analysed a new product-pod called the Perfect Nanny that can get in sync with a group and increase the happiness of its customers. The cost of this new product has not yet been disclosed. What differentiates this machine from robots?'

'I see you've done your homework.'

'I once interviewed a group of developers of an artificially intelligent "duck" that could restore hearing to the deaf with the help of sound waves.'

'Restoring people's hearing using electrodes is a mere trifle compared to the capabilities of our innovation,' Hoffman sniggered. Ever the promoter, he had transformed the modest office space rented for interviews with the press into a showroom.

'We are offering an experimental model developed along the same lines as those used by Rodney Brooks,' Simon explained. 'His article "Flesh and Machines" created a real stir back in the day: "We will be robots in part ourselves, while also being inseparably tied to them."'

'What you're referring to is a small group of people with shared interests, isn't that so? Are you also allowing for political interests and those of radical groups? I recently heard that terrorists have been attaching explosives to balloons. Is that one of the skills your smart machine can teach people?'

Hoffman shot his interlocutor a condescending look. 'Remind me, young man – what did you say your name was?'

'Peter Schutz.'

'I have to disappoint you, I'm afraid. The creators of the smart machine are a long way from being military types. We are make-believe artists, celestial beings, and children of kindness, love, and peace. Needless to say, a range of pain parameters for the group is included in the monitoring system for the Perfect Nanny. It will ensure you and your children don't prick your fingers on a poisoned spindle.'

Hoffman put down his Montblanc pen, set it aside and beckoned Schutz over to a window that overlooked the azure waters of a swimming pool. Around the thermal spring of the Blue Lagoon, set against the backdrop of the rosy sky, was a thick ring of petrified volcanic stones. From the showroom window, the spring spread out before the visitor as though it were in the palm of their hands. Schutz gazed fixedly at the warm water, where the audience was unhurriedly moving to and fro in bathing costumes while awaiting his presentation. A lady of a certain age with a beehive hairdo and heavy jewellery was trying to attract the attention of an infant whose protruding lips were covered in chocolate. Some of the contents of her glass spilled into the water. At the side of the pool, a woman with model looks was being rhythmically massaged by an Asian fellow wearing make-up as her chest moved up and down in unison with her airbed.

Next to her was a lad who vaguely resembled the janitor from his college and had come over from Tennessee, the 'Volunteer State', to earn some money. Everyone used to goad him about his peculiar way of slinking around the corridors of the college like an eel; only his seductive, almond-shaped eyes had earned him any praise. Hoffman caught sight of a beautiful woman wearing a thick, white mineral mask before some whirling steam momentarily hid the Blue Lagoon from view.

'What would you say all these people have in common?' Schutz turned away from the window to meet Hoffman's beaming smile. He had returned to the point where they had begun their conversation and picked up an object from the table: the Montblanc pen with the golden lid. Charles de Gaulle had signed documents with such a pen. He focused his gaze on it as Hoffman held it in his hand.

'I don't think I can answer that.'

'The answer's obvious. Every one of them wants to be happy. As you can see, the whole universe serves this purpose. Our innovativeness is merely one of the manifestations of potential engineering to calculate the optimum path to happiness based on a useful exchange formula. Please take a seat!'

'Thank you. What exactly is happiness for the developer of an artificially intelligent Perfect Nanny?'

'Pleasure that can be paid for. What is it for you, may I ask – something different?'

'The absence of pain. When the pain goes away, you always feel a deceptive sense of paradise.' Schutz sat down again. 'I have a provocative question for you. In your formula for happiness, do you take the price of life into account?'

Hoffman chuckled, not letting his guard down for an instant. This Schutz was not as simple as he looked. He decided it was time to pause the interview for a commercial break. 'Would you like to know how much the new product costs? The Perfect Nanny will soon be available to a wide circle of consumers. It's not something we strive to do, to work with the military – we're merely satisfying the demand in the mass market. The presentation will begin in a quarter of an hour's time when the price will be announced. Why don't you join the party in the Blue Lagoon?'

A cat that had been sitting as still as a statue on top of a sound system meowed and jumped off. When Hoffman put the pen on the glass table top, however, Schutz failed to take the hint. He set the folder of press releases down on the table and picked up the pen with the expensive lid, pointing it at the animal. He had guessed right. There was a remote control inside the pen; the cat was only a demonstration copy. When the gold cap was pressed, the cat went 'offline' and broke down like a child's toy. It fell onto the floor with a loud smack.

'Something akin to a robot that knows the temperature on a thermostat, whose modelled brain picks up both discrete and constant signals,' Schutz surmised. 'It can assemble and disassemble itself in a modular manner. I expect it's fitted with a video camera and a microphone. It appears there's no recording being made at the moment. Spot on!' He was beaming like a Christmas tree decoration made of brand-new superconductors. 'So that's what the showpiece and main exhibit of the Hoffman Museum is! The interview is over, Hoffman. I wish you a pleasant evening!'

The Blue Lagoon was suddenly plunged into darkness as the emergency siren howled. Hoffman realised his adversary had outwitted him as he stood groaning in the dark.

'What are you trying to prove? I will destroy you! To what

god do you pray, damn it?'

'To Schrödinger's Cat,' Schutz joked, and it seemed to Hoffman that he flashed a smile at him through the dark.

Unable to restrain himself, Hoffman leapt at him, pounding his fists. 'You idiot! You've shut down my presentation model and the whole system! How do you expect to get away with this?'

Schutz stepped aside, and Hoffman collapsed onto the floor, tripping over a little table. Now he was feverishly thinking about whether the people beside the geyser could hear him, where panic had broken out. Schutz realised the time had come to say goodbye. He could of course have made the finale to his visit equally as artistic – by flying out of his office window onto the square beside the pool, for instance, before doing a backwards somersault into the water and disappearing into the thermal springs. It was not unknown for him to indulge in a bit of flair, and at times he loved to make an impression on those around him with such circus tricks, but instead, he chose to leave the office in a business-like fashion, quickly and noiselessly. Only one lamp was lit in the murky corridor as the door slammed shut.

Hoffman was beside himself with rage. He had fallen for the boy's charms and allowed him to sabotage the presentation. The backup generator kicked in, and a computer came on. The face of the pool administrator popped up on the screen, warning him that there was some alarm by the pool but the technical support team was already trying to restore the power. The face politely asked whether everything was okay. Hoffman barked that he would have to announce the cancellation of the presentation and pay a hefty charge.

'An ass astride another ass,' he growled in Russian. 'You are a little vexed, Hoffman. Take a sedative!'

The virtual voice of Lu informed the assembled guests

outside that the technical operations at the Blue Lagoon were complete. There were shouts of delight – the audience in the pool had taken the difficulties to be part of the show. As the lights came on again, a beautiful Asian woman suddenly appeared in the room. Her body was decorated with a tattoo: a circle surrounded by flames. She had just emerged from the springs, and her hair was still wet. She drew closer to him, moving like a cat and staring into his eyes as though trying to hypnotise him even before her first words were out of her mouth.

'Putting yourself forward in place of an experienced model? I didn't think you were capable of such sacrifices.'

Hoffman scowled. 'I fear the general public is not yet ready to look upon a Schrödinger's Cat that takes the form of an Asian woman with a microchip inside her.'

She laughed. 'Then all that remains is for you to cover the compensation for the technical costs.' She waved in the direction of the deactivated cat and inspected Peter Schutz's accreditation card.

'I've never met this fellow before. Who is he? Some young upstart?'

'A madman! His name is probably just as false as his accreditation! He took the Meander synchronisation console and left. He'll pay for this,' Hoffman seethed.

'Don't worry! This situation will merely attract the right people's attention and raise the stakes to no end. Especially now. The biological engineering has appeared at the forefront. You need to find TRANSITION KEEPER…'

'Me? And what the hell is that anyway? A human?'

'A training programme created by New Babylon. It has a unique recognition system, one that recognises not only video but also voices, behaviour, and medical and biological indicators. It's not a vast amount of money. TRANSITION KEEPER will know all about the Meander by tomorrow.' Lu flipped her wet hair back, and her eyes shone with a steady gleam. She leaned over him and peered at the screen. 'Hebb's Law is the same for all neural networks. Each time the right decision is taken, the corresponding neural networks grow stronger, and each time the neurons successfully complete a task, the electrical connections grow stronger. It's a pretty strange selection – ninety-nine candidates if we use your formula, all of the female sex. We must find her before the others do. Don't you find this inspiring?'

'Not at all. I think there's a link between the world of people and the guy who disrupted my presentation.'

'Just let me prove it, Hoffman!' Lu took out the Meander. 'I've still got a spare prototype. It's worked consistently and remotely since we checked it. We need to synchronise with the workings of TRANSITION KEEPER's mind and take out everything she's got in her head.'

'You're taking a risk. The Meander's signal could easily be discovered.' Schutz had taken its remote control with him, and Hoffman's anxiety was rising once again. 'Don't you dare apply its influence now we could be on the verge of signing a deal!'

'I'll have only two attempts. I think I know who TRANSITION KEEPER might be. Children, I should check.'

Grumbling, Hoffmann pulled out a similar device in the form of a notebook. Lu walked out of the room, leaving the deactivated demonstration model with him. He entered Peter Schutz's photo and a capital 'F' in the command line to the best-verified playmates before turning on the Meander's tracking system, selecting the Interference and Annihilation mode. The visit from Lu had left a troubling aftertaste. She was too self-assured, knew too much and could do too much, and she had stopped seeking his approval for her actions altogether.

After Lu's death, Hoffman got a phone call. 'I am interested in purchasing the device,' said an unknown voice at the other end. *Her death has led to more problems and not fewer*, he thought, making his way to the spot where the second Meander's signal had last arisen from his computer screen. Hoffman had followed the second signal from the Meander in Portugal. The Marian apparition above the Douro had made him alter his plans dramatically, and now the circumstances on the embankment had forced him to go offline. His computer screen was cracked, from which the second Meander had now disappeared. He cursed as he stepped over the people on the embankment, who were kneeling and crossing themselves as they looked up at the sky. As he headed to the place where he had last seen the Meander's signal, elbowing his way towards the hotel entrance, he had caught sight of a dark-haired young man slipping out of the Eurostars Porto Duoro hotel, who was instantly recognisable on account of his deft movements and the stern gaze in his eyes, which were as black as raisins – traits that suggested that within him lurked a creature ready to get back in the game at any moment. Hoffman had seen him among the guests at the presentation at the Blue Lagoon two days before. Meanwhile, the apparition had dissolved into nothingness. The most likely scenario was that some positive interference had occurred that had contributed to his experiments getting well and truly out of control.

EARLIER – GIOVANNI

Sometime before, a man carrying a cage with a brightly patterned shawl thrown over it had appeared in Old Chiswick in the Reverend's courtyard, collecting signatures. He was an immigrant who knew a great deal about dogs and indicated he would be willing to look after His Grace's beasts should the latter ever have to leave them on their own while he was out of town. Upon being ordered to leave the premises immediately, the cheeky young man had revealed that he knew all about the Reverend's family secrets – those secrets His Grace did not want to be taken outside the temple walls. By way of proof, he held out a photograph of the Reverend's son. All he wanted in return, he added, was to be allowed to work for him.

'That's all you want from me?' the Reverend repeated.

At that moment, a strange grunting noise was heard from the covered cage that was now resting on the ground beside them.

The man tore off the colourful shawl, and a pair of frightened creatures looked out at the Reverend from inside it: a brown miniature pig and a golden Pekingese. He eagerly held out the documents he had received the previous day and continued to set out his 'diplomatic' demands.

'Under local laws, pigs aren't afforded the same rights as canines, but they can be taken for walks with other dogs.'

'Young man, are you lobbying for the interests of a representative of the ancient Chinese breed and "the gentleman who pays the rent" who is trained to find truffles? Show me their registration documents!'

The Reverend decided to temporarily postpone his telephone call to the General to ask for help and agree to conduct this social experiment with the immigrant. 'I have three dogs,' he declared.

'A Peruvian Crested Dog and two Italian greyhounds, far superior to any others in this part of London. Will you be able to cope with them all?' He became lost in thought. 'What is your name?'

'Giovanni.'

Old Chiswick, London

Giovanni couldn't believe it. Was Fortune smiling upon him once again? He had no interest in Hoffman's waffling, who thought he ruled the world. He had been waiting for a good offer until, for the first time, he spied the face of Fortune, which turned out to be the face. Simon and Fitz had left California on the same flight as him, who had been divided from them only by the curtain between economy and business class. During the flight, he overheard a conversation about the young man's mother, Margaret Evans, and his priest father. The person who called himself Hoffman had slept in the chair next to him throughout the entire flight. When they landed, he knew what to do. He needed to get a job working for the Reverend. Hoffman role.

And now a stranger was sitting beside him and offering him an incredible deal for the truth about Fitz and his mother.

'The Reverend has a right to know the truth about them both,' declared Giovanni.

Life is full of inventions.

'We can continue this conversation when the money is in my account.'

Giovanni remained opposite the obelisk pondering these strange circumstances until a message about the transaction came through on his phone. *Could it really be the case that the cost of living comes down to how much you're willing to pay for the face of your Fortune?* he wondered as he made his way to the temple.

At the Reverend's home, he found His Grace examining a

new collection of artworks by Dominic Harris that depicted some of the world's most intriguing bird species, among which a puffin had caught his eye. Giovanni told him about the new Lucia Santos returning to visit a temple in northern Portugal. When he noticed a fold at the corner of the Reverend's lips like a barb on the stem of a flower, his ears pricked up. Aware that the two Italian greyhounds and Peruvian Crested Dog were watching him, he lowered his head so as not to meet the animals' gaze.

'Don't you want to take a look? Maybe it looks like a miracle, but it's true. The face in the sky and Lucia Santos's face are the same.'

'Thank God!' The Reverend tried to pull the photos closer for a better view. An angry grimace distorted his face.

Fearing the old man might be having a heart attack, Giovanni opted not to put all his cards on the table. 'Would you like me to light some joss sticks, or perhaps you would prefer a drop of your favourite gin?'

'No, I'd prefer it if you brought me my favourite travel bag. I need to see the General.'

'Do you want me to accompany you on your journey?' Giovanni had never dared hope that everything would go so smoothly.

'No, not this time,' the Reverend replied thoughtfully. 'Hurry up and pack my things! The departure is scheduled for early tomorrow morning.'

Inwardly jubilant at the fact that His Grace would be leaving the next day, Giovanni scurried out to prepare the bag so that he could leave it in a visible place in the living room. On his way out, he touched one of Harris's digital artworks that depicted a number of beautiful bouquets of roses in vases. The flowers on the digital canvas started to fall, and the perfume of falling petals began to fill the Temple of Dogs.

Carinthia, Austria

On returning to his hotel, Simon was not expecting any news. He had obtained exhaustive evidence about Lo but he had learned nothing about Lu. It was Margaret's voice on the recording. Suddenly, however, the old-fashioned telephone—an antique—rang behind the bar. The barman handed him the receiver.

'It's for you!'

The voice at the other end of the line was unfamiliar. 'It's good to hear your voice, my friend. Did you like what you found on the Chinese paper near the swan house?'

'Who is this? Do I know you?'

'You can call me Taylor.'

Simon turned around to find the barman had disappeared from view so he was able to speak freely. 'I'm aware of the experiments with stem cells performed by Doris Taylor from the University of Minnesota, the Taylor at the Pentagon, and Frederick Winslow Taylor. Which one are you?'

'I'm the one who knows a thing or two about port and every brand in Gaio, but now's not the time to discuss my business.'

'Listen, Taylor, I'm guessing that, since you took the trouble of calling, it wasn't to discuss a suit.'

'You've just been to the swan house. Did you find Margaret Evans?'

'What do you know about Miss Evans? Have you met her there?'

'The last time I saw her in your company was at Westminster

Abbey. The three of us were attending an organ recital. You wouldn't have said no to the idea of taking a stroll with her beneath the giant sequoias in Bodnant Garden in Wales. I must admit, Simon, my rules for living are somewhat different from your romantic approach to courting women.'

'So, it was you who did the performance with the Chinese vases near the swan house, gave me the rhyme on Chinese paper and brought Bill Miller to me?'

'The riddle of the fifteenth stone in the Japanese Garden of Ryōan-ji was solved. The machine had given the TRANSITION KEEPER value to Margaret Evans.'

'Do you work for the General? Are you on the General's yacht right now in neutral waters?'

'Your guess is only half-right. I'm in neutral waters on a modest rented vessel called the *Princess*. My job is to protect the only daughter of the General and Margaret, and the Wings of the Angels, who create the best stories in the world. If this answer of mine is to your liking …'

'So, the General and Margaret have a daughter?'

'Yes, and it was her idea to leave the puzzle in the swan house.' Taylor had shown that he was fully abreast of all matters concerning the private life of Margaret Evans and her loved ones. 'I daresay that Fitz has already won a chess match against one of the St Germain brothers.'

'No, Taylor. He has merely put him in checkmate with his rook.'

'Simon, I have a different task at hand: to warn you that the time has come to put Margaret's son into the General's care. I have a notepad with a Meander built into it, one that bears a strong resemblance to the formula that is troubling you. So now two people are in danger,' Taylor warned him.

'You mean to say that what I've been doing for him isn't enough?'

'At your request, he went off to Britain. What difference does it make what the stone in the Ryan-ji garden is if you have solved the riddle itself?'

Simon had no idea why, but he was increasingly taking a liking to this man from nowhere.

'I wish to warn you that I do not meddle in real events. Should you be interested in further participation in financial and political games, I would have no objection. Don't you think it's high time we worked together, Simon? Will you join forces with me? The likes of you and I are going to be at an advantage because we will be serving humankind rather than the military or the government. Saving the whole of humanity is impossible, but one can save a single person. Margaret, the real Margaret, might have held onto her life if for no other reason than I wasn't the only one who thought her behaviour might have differed from the machine's tasks.'

Taylor provided the coordinates of the yacht before disappearing from Simon's life as unexpectedly as he had appeared in it. Stefan reappeared to put the old telephone back in its usual place. He pointed towards the taxi rank.

Simon went upstairs to his room at the top of the hotel. On the recording Miller had given him, he heard two female voices and some well-spoken English. The first voice was Miller's daughter; the second was Margaret's.

'You look like a real lady, Miss Evans.'

'And you look all grown-up and more beautiful, Lo. The course of therapy at the camp did you good. They want to see you at home.'

'No way.'

'Is your tattoo a symbol of love?'

'Yes. Do you like it?'

'What's her name?'

'It's a secret.'

'I was pretty sure it would be. Will you introduce me to her?'

'Yes, tomorrow. On condition that we play a game. If I win, half goes to you. Agreed?'

'I agree. Only I don't get it – what game are you and your friend playing at exactly?'

'Guessing people's thoughts for money.'

'Guessing people's thoughts is the start of self-destruction.'

'There are other games she and I play too. I'll introduce you to her tomorrow like I say. Only she mustn't see your face. Let's go upstairs – I'll show you what I bought during the city festival. In the travel bag, you'll find some powder. You must hide your face with it.'

'Laura, the clothing in the back is from the Muromachi period. Probably a wedding kimono for a young woman.'

'That's for the game. You must come wearing it tomorrow, agreed? It's going to be fun; I promise you!'

A few hours later, there was a phone call to Margaret's room. It was Taylor's voice.

'Margaret? Laura is dead. You must leave this place at once! The city will soon be shut off. You are Leiko Oshima. Your documents are under the door.'

Simon pictured Margaret putting on young Laura's kimono and powdering her face as she transformed herself into Leiko Oshima until she was unrecognisable. She had slipped out of the hotel, looking down at the floor at all times—exactly as a Japanese woman was supposed to—and a day later had reached her destination safe and sound in soul and body. In the belt of her obi, Margaret had found Laura's note on the Chinese paper. No one knew whether it was a game or whether Laura had genuinely sensed the danger emanating from her friend, but one way or another Margaret had agreed that the General had serious grounds for keeping her hidden from the outside world.

Simon called the General's number. The room in the old hotel filled with his booming voice. The General was in high spirits.

'Are you still in Austria? Did you decide to check on the police's work for yourself? Commendable eagerness! I've got some good news. Your hypothesis has been confirmed. I've been sent the coordinates for a Black Cloud – it looks like Hoffman's big game. The Black Cloud was integrated with other clouds and a database of thousands of people, but we have managed to identify the playmates in the transaction…'

'That's useful for the OSCE[27] but not for me. There was a well-known dead journalist in the database.'

'Yes, there was, Simon. How did you discover him?'

'He was working for me, just like Margaret Evans' son.'

'Hmm. Then I'll tell you the key things you need to know. During the presentation in Iceland, the term TRANSITION KEEPER was put into the search engine. It turns out you were right: Hoffman took an interest in her too.'

'General, I have solved the mystery of TRANSITION KEEPER. She and Margaret Evans are one and the same person. And you knew it the whole time!'

---

[27] The Organization for Security and Co-operation in Europe and the world's largest security-oriented intergovernmental organisation, whose 57 participating countries are located in Europe, Northern and Central Asia, and North America.

'New Babylon has excellent taste. And you and I were right to have created the TRANSITION KEEPER programme. It has brought results. The greatest mystery lies in a woman's own attempt to understand herself—not as dictated by men. I have never met any woman who would go as far to pursue this goal as Margaret Evans has.'

The General was clearly in good form today.

'Is that why you turned Margaret into your own Irish colony for ten long years?'

'Simon, due to certain extraordinary circumstances, she was forced to become a sort of Japan, spending many years isolated from the rest of the world.'

'I can ascertain those circumstances from you directly, General.'

'Right now, Margaret Evans is a very special instrument for preventing terrorist attacks. And a very effective one, let me tell you, given that in just a couple of days, she has managed to calculate something that for you has been mere conjecture and guesswork for so long!'

'Do you know what I was thinking about? How it's unlikely we will see one another in the near future, General. I wish to say goodbye.'

'Well, then. You are mending your ways.'

'Margaret's son needs your help.'

'Check for an equivalent transaction in Iceland! Fischer's restaurant?'

There was a pause.

'Since when have you been looking after him?'

'Ever since Margaret disappeared I wasn't sure whether his mother was alive or dead. He is now in Iceland for a meeting today with representatives of Reporters without Borders. The name he is going by at the moment is Peter Schutz.'

'I see the transaction in the Black Cloud. Look for it there! I will take care of Fitz.'

Simon boarded the train and before long arrived safely at Munich Airport's departure lounge. News of the Dresses app's involvement in the explosion was being broadcast on every TV screen. He made a call to Liz, who had just returned from her meeting with Fitz in Old Harbour.

'I find it hard to believe that what's going on in the world is work of Hoffman's hands. My children play that Dresses game,' she told him.

'Is Fitz somewhere nearby?'

'No. I thought you were supposed to take care of it.'

Simon thought about Fitz's mother. The sun was setting on the runway and lighting up the aerodrome. The huge aircraft were sleeping. No one was about. Two abandoned silver staircases served as a reminder of the dream that had not come true.

TRANSITION KEEPER

TRANSITION KEEPER looked at the symbol – the sign of the Japanese military and the imperial seal – and switched to non-linear calculations, entering into a conversation with the technical communications systems in order to establish a dialogue with the Boeing 7 jet as it flew. She identified the subject on board the Boeing and cross-checked him against the video and voice records available to her. It was Augustin Hoffman. TRANSITION KEEPER sent the details of the aircraft and the name of one of the passengers for Shanghai.

The Secret Room, London

The General opened the door to the Austrian guest house that had become the cornerstone of his existence with Margaret Evans. After splitting up with her, he had once paid a special visit to the house out of curiosity to get a sense of the space of her life without him. The clouds had been low over the land that day, and from the windows of her home, all that could be seen was an enormous rosebush speckled with large red and white roses. *My Margaret lives in the clouds* was all he could think as he surveyed the interior, which was more like a Tudor pile than a guest house worth a million Euros. Certain objects reminded the General of the accoutrements at Mrs Levers' gallery at Sun Light Harbour: the Wedgwood porcelain dinner services with their unique colours, from queen's wax and black basalt to jasper; the Venetian coloured glasses with their amazing twists; the silver rings around the waists of the napkins; the antique candleholders. A collection of fine wines hidden behind the high glass of some thick wooden cabinets distracted him a little from his memories. The General could easily imagine the starched and gleaming Claudia Barbari tablecloth adorned with lace and ribbons, who once declared, 'True luxury is the ability to spend time with the ones we love and who love us!'

Wondering how much noise and happy hubbub this house might have held had life continued in the same manner, he waited a while longer on the terrace overlooking the lake as the white clouds gave way to a picturesque view of the local scenery. Fog fluctuates in mountainous regions, but that day the tiny village had been utterly swamped by a basin of clouds that only dispersed when the General was a long way off on the road home. Once he had driven far away from the guest house, a soothing sun shone in the sky.

The General's daughter had been born early in the morning, symbolising her arrival in the world the Land of the Rising Sun. The midwife at the local clinic had frozen in wonderment, so unusual was the colour of her eyes when she had opened them for the first time. One couldn't quite say what the colour was. The little girl had not cried, and her mother had been frightened, thinking she had been born blind. Then, at that moment, a bird had begun singing melodiously outside the guest house, and the little girl with the mother-of-pearl eyes had responded to it with a call of her own. As they opened wide to the world, the expression on her face had become extraordinarily grown-up.

'It looks as though the child has perfect hearing and vision,' the midwife had assured her.

In her, for her father, were the pearls of all the waters of the world and all the light reflected by every aeroplane in the high sky. The General had tasked Margaret with choosing a name. She had not thought about it for long and decided to place her faith in Lewis Carroll rather than the Holy Scriptures, to which the General had made no objection. Margaret was no ordinary woman, as he must have known when Alice was born. After her return, however, Margaret had been greatly changed, and the child, rather than softening her heart, had only made her cold reasoning more categorical.

'Margaret! No one, not even my smart machine, knows exactly from whom the threat came. Let's not tell the child who her real mother is! You know better than anyone how I feel about war. My life is formed from the lives and deaths of specific people, often people close to me, and I would hate to put you and the child in danger, he had told her fervently.

'Do you know what I think? You are probably right – real life is a threat to which one must know how to respond. I'll see you with the children somewhere deep in the British countryside – Llandudno in Wales, where Oxford tutors love to spend their summers – or at Birr Castle. But even Ireland isn't safe now. I shall choose her a house that has a history to which she can return, where I shall have gardens of my own to tend. Beneath its windows will grow bushes with big white and red roses. Whenever I look at them, I shall recall a line of verse by the Tudor poet John Skelton: *Here I shall lay out my gardens.*'

Sometimes he thought that this was what love for a woman was all about. 'Have you chosen the Perfect Nanny candidate for our child? Everything will be as we agreed.'

'The nanny? She will be in my place now, and she will become your new album of peace, General.'

After visiting the guest house beneath whose windows, he had scattered his thorny twigs with petals from the rose bush, the General had created an exact replica of it. He had achieved a facsimile that was perfect in every way, except that not a single detail in its interior hinted at her, probably so as to wipe her from his memory. He had not changed anything about his life for ten long years.

The ebony door to the virtual space of the guest house in the Secret Room closed. The General summoned Richard and gave him his final instructions regarding the virtual doors. He vividly imagined his meeting with Fitz and his daughter. On the way to the aerodrome, Richard filled in the General on the latest news. Alfonso had been telling fairy tales to all and sundry, saying that he knew about the chest and a little girl who had the key to it – even though the chaplain had given him strict orders not to tell anyone about her. 'Let him chatter all he likes – no one will believe a word of it. People love fairytales,' the General answered.

On the morning of day seven of the Transition, when the General left the Secret Room, all the tasks on his to-do list were completed. He gazed out of the aeroplane window, thinking about the other world and whether it really existed. 'It undoubtedly exists. It's just that it's harder to recognise beneath a layer of dust and dirt. But it is there, that other world,' he said out loud, catching sight of changes in the celestial map laid out before him. Some of the snow-white clouds, their tips giving off the barest hint of colour, were gleaming with that white effulgence that is so hard to find on Earth. Recognisable forms took shape here and there. The General sometimes tried to predict when they were going to appear and, when he succeeded, he would think that, were he a god looking at the earth from the ethers, he would have grave doubts about whether it was worth combining the architectural languages of the celestial and the terrestrial. Breathing this pattern alone was enough for him. Life was like air: it incorporated factors of impermanence and imbalance that depended on the thickness of clouds and the strength of the wind gusting over the surface of the earth.

As we move about the earth, we are merely data values and symbols of those we love here in the heavens, he thought as the plane flew towards the Sinai Peninsula on the border between Asia and Africa. He looked down on sheer drops between the clouds that were like bottomless white wells.

Returning to the Secret Room, Richard opened up a notepad with a flashing Meander on it that had been delivered to him in

Margaret's name and examined it carefully. He was expecting to see columns of accounting figures attesting to the financial transactions involving Hoffman or records made in the Japanese Hiragana and Romaji writing systems, but there were no lists of contacts or clues at all. The light on the Meander went out. He found a remote control shaped like a torpedo on the desk with which he opened an ebony door to the Archival Room. Behind them were only a switched-off monitor, some books wrapped in crumpled postal paper and bearing Austrian stamps depicting a bird, and two photos. From one of them, Margaret Evans smiled out with a young priest standing beside her, while the other was a photo of a young man. Beside them lay a note stating that the General's long-standing feud with Bill Miller about whether or not Margaret Evans was innocent of Laura's death had ended in a draw. Miller's beloved wife, Sarah, had died several years earlier at a clinic for the blind. Bill had asked the General to see to it that no one ever found out about this.

Richard closed the ebony doors in the Secret Room.

The Sinai Peninsula (Territory of the Former Mesopotamia)

Alice loved to look down from an aircraft window on a sunny day as her plane and its shadow came together to form a single whole when it landed. On the approach to the Sinai Peninsula, she recalled the border zone between the land and the sea that had influenced US military strategy during the Cold War. She compared the rational and ordered European landscape with the silver of the rivers, the horizons, and the trigonometry of the white steel wind turbines, taking in a view of the water flowing onto the dry land. The Red Sea and the shore were divided into two compositions: one populated by bathers and lines of buoys; the other embellished with multicoloured beach umbrellas, the white-as-snow right angles of the lighthouses, and the geometrical figures of the piers cutting into the water. The holidaymakers were being displaced by gigantic platforms in the sea with a theme park, restaurants, and hotels.

In the terminal building at the airport, Alice was met by a stately man with a magnificent British accent and a beard, whom everyone referred to with the utmost respect as the General. On making her acquaintance, he gave her a gift of a poetry-covered shot glass, for which she thanked him by quoting a five-line poem by the Chinese Romantic poet Xu Zhimo. She was thinking about the connection between the conflict in Palestine, the Suez Crisis, and Operation Musketeer, which had ended with the secret Protocol of Sèvres being drawn up between the governments of

Israel, France, and the United Kingdom. *I bet the General knows all the dotted lines of these connections*, she thought.

On the way to the beach, the General promised to take her on a deep-sea diving trip to explore shipwrecks and after that to the Cummings Science and Technology Park in Huntington. Alice was curious to take a look at a military site where spacecraft and rockets were tested. On the table beside the deckchair, he set down a vase decorated with a big cherry—an exotic fruit in their part of the world—and some golden tea.

'It is the Egyptians who call it golden and use seeds and fruit instead of leaves for good health,' she observed.

In Alice's dream, the sunlight was penetrating a thick layer of red water, turning the sun's rays into an underwater continent where she saw shoals of multicoloured fish and, in the depths, a Napoleon fish. She tied a rope to her foot so that the waves would not wash her onto the coral reef, observing the lilac shadows. It was an extraordinary feeling being one with the fish. Some of them swam up to her to tickle her thigh, while others, somewhat larger, skulked in the murky deep, their scales shimmering. 'Just don't let yourself be carried away!' she heard Lady Swan's voice singing...

General *tickled* her heel. Alice goggled. He perched on the edge of the deckchair and tickled her heel till she giggled. How long had it been since she'd felt anything like that? He thought of Alice as the paradox of his smart machine Meanwhile, a group of teenagers was asking a self-learning machine questions in order to hone its skills. Alice's own enquiry to the machine boiled down to a single question in twelve languages: *If God were to decide today to make himself a machine, to whom would He give supremacy – man or a sum of values?* Related to this was the question of which tool the machine would choose in order to find out how the living world works, she reflected.

'You won first prize in NASA's junior essay contest for the best self-learning machine question. Did you surprise your teachers and Nanny?' the General began.

'Nanny is not interested in such topics as "Life's Secrets Have Nothing to Do with Quantum". Life for her means domestic cleanliness and a good salary. You won't be returning me to her, will you?'

'Half mirrors,' answered Alice. And the crispness of the lines to get an answer to any question.

'The poetic reference may have grown old,' the General replied. 'The machine composed that line from the poem itself, abiding by the rules of Xu Zhimo's Chinese grammar.'

'William Butler Yeats himself alluded to it. Do you admire his "Aedh Wishes for the Cloths of Heaven"?'

'Now it's my turn. My mother? Is it important for me to know now, when the world is rushing into the abyss in the multiplicity of imaginary angles, circles, and mirror constructions?'

They were interrupted by some soldiers.

'We are looking for Miss Evans. Do you happen to know where she is? A military dispatch has come through with orders for her arrest,' one barked.

'As you can see, Margaret is not here. Go back to whomever it was sent you!' the General shot back. He turned towards some Egyptian policemen coming into view a short distance behind them as the soldiers hovered, apparently unsure whether to approach or retreat. 'And another thing – send your boss to see me! That's an order!' he shouted.

It was obvious to the General that there were now people out there who were very interested in TRANSITION KEEPER's unique capabilities. Given that members of the British government were proposing to invest vast sums in a super machine, that was hardly surprising, he reasoned. What did the Americans know about it? Surely the government wasn't already aware of it and on edge? No major threatening incidents had occurred during the Transition, aside from an official request that had come in from the Paris office of Reporters Without Borders and a secret report about a false alarm on board a Boeing that was attributed to just another system malfunction. Both events took place yesterday.

'There's a phone call for you,' the soldier informed him, interrupting his train of thought.

'On a secure line?' The General moved a short distance away from them. 'Why are you looking for Miss Evans?'

'Yesterday, an airliner sent a false alarm signal due to a malfunction in the programme. There was a passenger on board who said he knew of your secret TRANSITION KEEPER. This is the woman, Margaret Evans. His name is Hoffman.'

'Maybe he saw Margaret Evans in the sky and heard her virtual voice a day ago?'

'Spot on! He maintains that Margaret Evans is working for you. Is that true?'

'A little earlier there was a signal from Reykjavik that she had been seen in Reykjavik, but thought to be a ghost. I knew that woman once. If I come across her, I shall certainly let you know. The General let out a deep sigh as the blockhead of a soldier glanced at the girl. 'Alice is currently giving lessons in etiquette. She's teaching soldiers how to pour golden tea correctly.' He handed the phone back to them, who had received their orders. It crossed his mind that he would quite like to find out where Margaret was right now too.

Alice and the General were left alone by the shore. 'Now everyone is trying to get on the trail of the playmates and wants to know who discovered the threat and does not fit into the linear computations,' she said.

There were no visitors left on the Red Sea coast. A pair of drones hovered in the air above them before changing course.

Soon the cells of the machine, like the blood vessels in a living system, will be filled with new information and conclusions about connections invisible to the human eye and incomprehensible to the human mind, and it will once again see an image that gives it inspiration and confidence in the future, the General thought. He looked up to the sky as he often did when he didn't know the answers to simple questions, as though appealing to the Almighty with his feet rooted to the earth. Integral to the elemental forces in the uneasy sky above the peninsula were sham edifices, formulae, perfect hearing and taste, pretension, and deceptive daydreams – at least for those who can read the language of the sky and have at some time ventured up there.

'It looks as though balance has been restored to the world,' Alice surmised. 'What are you looking for up there? After all, there's no one there apart from the ones we love.'

The General looked at her in surprise.

'Look – there's someone down here!' Alice pointed at the silhouette of a young man approaching them along the shore who was wearing a Chinese tunic suit with a soldier's button. The seagulls, the only creatures able to fish in the Red Sea without breaking any laws, fell silent. A roar of thunder was heard, and it began to drizzle. The figure called to Alice, looking cheerful. For his part, Fitz had the same smile as Lady Swan about whom Alice had reminisced for so many years.

'Alice, this is your half-brother and Miss Evans's son,' the General announced.

'So I've got a sister?' Fitz pondered.

'Then is she a changeling?' someone asked.

The General peered anxiously at the boulders from behind which the Reverend had emerged.

'We've got a real Saint Nicholas of Myra on our hands,' His Grace smiled. He was holding a woman's revolver. 'I'm your father, Fitz,' he muttered quickly.

Alice took a step forward. 'You used to know his mum?'

'So that was why you needed your machine god? So that you could steal my son from me!' the Reverend cried, accusingly.

'Which one?' the General responded.

The Reverend didn't fire, Fitz made a powerful sound, and he fell over. As Fitz and Alice rushed towards him, a wave from the Red Sea knocked him to the ground. He scrambled to his feet, but when he and the soldiers reached the boulders, they found nothing save the waves washing over the old man's fedora. The Reverend's body had vanished. The rain stopped as though it had never happened. A kind of trigonometry established itself in the sky.

DAY SEVEN

Neutral Waters
On Board the *Princess*

'Am I in heaven or hell?' the Reverend moaned. Margaret removed the pain syndrome.

'Oh, Margaret, it's you! I thought I was in a registry office. So, I'm alive?'

'Indeed, you are. Your sin is no reason to depart this mortal coil, Your Grace!'

'You are in neutral waters,' muttered an unfamiliar male voice. 'Mild drowsiness and a single, solitary scratch. You tried to shoot yourself in the head but missed. People like you often overestimate their abilities. Stay here and rest while we go up on deck.'

'Can you explain to me how I got on board?'

Vibration changed.

'I picked you up on the shore. Someone needed to stop you from doing any more awful things, don't you think? My name is Taylor.'

'Are you the captain of this vessel?' the Reverend heard a girl's voice.

'Yes, ma'am.'

'Mr Taylor, you and the General saved my mother, but at the same time you proved powerless when it came to doing the same for another child.'

'Alice, saving the whole of humanity is impossible, but one can save a single person,' Taylor declared.

At that moment, they heard the sound of a fast and expensive yacht moving rapidly towards them. Even through the gloom, they could sense the vessel's style and speed. In the next moment, the General stepped aboard the princess.

'Greetings, Taylor. Have you seen the evidence?' he bellowed.

'I implemented TRANSITION KEEPER's "human factor protection" programme, but you walked out of the British Museum. A computer could create that so-called "Little Britain", the little palisades, and the swan house at the lake, anywhere. Are you hiding something from me?'

'Sorry, Taylor, but I'm no physicist or cyberneticist; my domain is defence. In my professional sphere, I'm accustomed to trusting the evidence. TRANSITION KEEPER performed its mission and sent the calculations to my machine and that was it. Margaret is just a backup copy, a record of the brain made by the computer Blue Gene[28] at an American military lab. She doesn't need you. Taylor, don't forget, you are Alice's protector.'

'The reason TRANSITION KEEPER has not yet become a dictator is that she has a demand for love that is of a different order altogether,' enthused Taylor. 'Your daughter has a big potential to become one. Ultimately, you can achieve precision when replicating the bodily casing and the human brain's reactions. But you can't replicate Fate.'

'You merely guarded Alice against external interference. I was disappointed when I found out about this. She took away all my drones and dragons…' go on the General.

---

[28] An IBM project aimed at designing supercomputers that can reach operating speeds in the petaFLOPS (PFLOPS) range with low power consumption. The project created three generations of supercomputers: Blue Gene/L; Blue Gene/P; and Blue Gene/Q.

'They are useless in a situation where we have practices for warning against and limiting threats.'

Their conversation was interrupted as the boat stirred into movement.

'Help!' came a voice.

'Good Lord, who's that?' exclaimed the General.

'Your cousin, the Reverend – who else?' replied Taylor.

'Thank you for pulling the Holy Father out of the water, Taylor. You are free. I will have a word with His Grace. And remember,' said the General as he descended, 'when there's a consensus about what the real world should be like, that world becomes extremely fragile!'

'The upcoming threat will be the biggest crisis since the days of the Third World War. Its consequences are going to be far graver than the global financial crisis,' Taylor couldn't resist predicting.

'Taylor, New Babylon has analysed the data. I told you everything,' answered the General, looking up and past him. The General headed towards the hatch.

The Reverend and the General crossed the deck together there was no one on board.

'But word has it that TRANSITION KEEPER controls your smart machine,' countered the Reverend, appearing out of nowhere. 'Let's go back to the Secret Room and discuss this matter.'

Then he and the General boarded the General's dark yacht.

It's all here: an exact copy of the Secret Room in London. Even the view out of the window. This cupola provides protection against a direct rocket strike.

The General pressed a button on the remote control in the cabin and some artworks in the same style as *Still Life with Animals* appeared on the walls of the Secret Room. The Reverend could not tear himself away from the paintings by Pieter Aertsen of an interior with tables laden with fruit and food, among which could be found a vase of flowers. 'I successfully sold my mini pigs to the Motobusk for truffle hunting,' he announced before turning his attention to the heart of the matter. 'Your "exceptional circumstances" are largely outside my understanding.'

The General shook his head and opened the doors to New Babylon screen. The Reverend saw an image of the Earth on the display.

'No changes at all to the training. There is only one risk factor: The machine has removed the former borders of military conflicts on the map of the world,' observed the Reverend and placed his empty glass on the torpedo-shaped coffee table. 'If her spirit is lingering in this room, it can only mean that the woman is alive.'

'Immortality was a condition of the TRANSITION KEEPER programme's existence.'

The Reverend began hiccupping as though he were suffering an allergic attack.

Fitz was asleep. In his dream, the plumy clouds were particularly expressive. He was trying to read what they were saying. Meanwhile, Alice was showing him a catkin in her palm.

'Lady Swan taught me that if you catch a big catkin in your hands, it means you're going to receive an important message.'

'But the only time you can catch them is in the spring,' he replied, blowing on the one she was holding till it flew up into the air.

'Be with me in spirit, Fitz! Anything is possible...'

'Then why doesn't Mum communicate with us?'

'Doesn't she? I talked to her all the time during the Transition. She warned me about the Dora River phenomenon and told me she didn't want to ruin the balance.'

'I've only seen her as a ghost since she left. I wasn't alone. Are you really interested in this problem of balance?'

'Answers to certain questions help to solve some issues. Right now, I'm more interested in the birth of the Dictator. Have you heard anything about him?'

'No, I've heard nothing.'

'Then what is it you want to know, Fitz?'

Fitz woke up. Flickering with a violet light on the little table, the notebook with the Meander pattern on the cover and Montblanc pen lay before him. Close by, Simon noticed he was awake.

'Simon, Holy Father?'

'Don't worry, Fitz. He is alive.'

'Ultimately, what are we left with?' he mused. 'The shot fired by the Reverend activated the bank account, but the transaction was blocked.'

'Neither of those two facts is proof of criminal activity,' Fitz concluded loudly. 'Whose account was this?'

'Giovanni's, the Reverend's assistant. He fled from the Temple of Dogs without taking anything with him except for an old black hat.'

'Is it his flight that concerns you?'

'Did the two cloned mini-pigs take the place of the champion's prize in the game?' Simon queried. 'I am sure that the TRANSITION KEEPER programme was responsible for a joke.'

'By the way, you have modelled Hoffman's instrument along the lines of the one that I took from Iceland.' Fitz pressed on the lid of a Montblanc fountain pen and pointed at the notebook.

'Look! Exactly the same thing happened in Iceland when those players attacked me.'

'We still haven't managed to establish their location.'

Fitz opened the notebook with the Meander. 'Come over here, Simon! What do you think? It looks like my sister's school exercise book. The sentences are short, clear, and concise. The language is German.'

'Something about red rooftops. Kids playing in the garden, and the disappointment of a political party. The piglets are pink. The emperor's new clothes are invisible,' Simon translated. 'What would your sister have to say about this?'

'She can read the water and wind.' Fitz began examining the cover of the notebook. 'So, there's no other notepad?'

'There are millions of notepads.'

'But only one of the pens is real?'

'Taylor established who Hoffman last spoke to on the phone before his meeting with Giovanni in London. He was interested in acquiring a device.'

At that moment, the coordinates of the Secret Room appeared among the pages of the notebook.

'The owner of another notebook wants to meet you,' declared Simon.

The Secret Room, London

'TRANSITION KEEPER continues to monitor the situation,' Richard remarked. The General loved his old servant more than anyone else who had ever worked for him. Today, however, the latter had hinted that he intended to hand in his notice. The General had not let his expression reveal that this news had hurt him deeply.

'I find out any news about Alice, General,' Richard said.

There's no need to worry. Your daughter is safe. Miller called.

'Get in touch with him, and you'll be near her.' Richard nodded.

'Why did you keep her hidden away for so long?' Miller asked.

The old man has really gone to seed. He has aged many years in the few days since Sarah's death, the General thought. He answered for him in a gentle tone.

'You know the reason full well, Miller.'

'Not so. She showed me a couple of tricks yesterday that I was delighted about. Her predictions came true. When she plays the game, her counting is good enough to compete with your quantum computer. She then discovered the whereabouts of a person named Giovanni who was interested in the Casket of Mazarin. I asked her to switch off all the CCTV cameras for a few minutes on her way out.'

The General glanced at Richard, who nodded in

confirmation. When the conversation was over, Richard invited him to go through into the Archives Room, where he switched on the three displays and enlarged their images.

'That's Alice at Miller's casino, based on information that came in today,' he commented.

'Do you think I'm unaware of all the difficulties that come with a time of transition like adolescence?' the General blurted out. 'Can you say with certainty where she is now?'

Richard shook his head. 'I doubt it. I went looking for your daughter in two places.' He pointed to a different display that showed an image featuring Alice as the face of an advertising campaign by a cosmetics brand. The product had broken all sales records in the sector. In the next image, Alice could be seen talking to a young man in a cathedral. 'Do you know that place?' he asked.

The General recognised the boy from the family of the Keepers of the Chest.

'I guess all the images of her were taken at the same time,' Richard speculated. 'One is a probability machine for games of poker; the other a perfect switch for consumer advertising.'

At that moment, a bell was heard. 'I forgot to tell you, General – Taylor asked me to pass on a message to you. He wanted you to set aside a little time for them.'

General can see Fitz and a man of Asian appearance outside the door to the Secret Room. 'Check the copies of Fitz! Call him in!' the General barked, pressing a button on the remote control until the still-life paintings of the Antwerp School were replaced by some Oriental vases.

When the two guests appeared, the Chinese visitor could not take his eyes off the collection of ancient porcelain. 'These are Chinese vases from Mr and Mrs Liver's collection,' he declared.

'They date from the eighteenth century – the Qualong Dynasty. Their secret has remained exactly that. In my collection, I have the very same sort of light-blue vases from the fifteenth century.'

The General scrutinised his visitor. 'Have we met before?' he asked.

'I know what was in the Chinese rhyme,' said the Chinese guest with restraint.

'This is the first time I have visited London. I have heard a great deal about the return of El Greco's artworks to Toledo Cathedral thanks to a smart machine.' He held the Reverend's gaze unblinkingly. 'I am very keen on one of his paintings: *The Disrobing of Christ*.'

It was immediately apparent that Fitz was not in on the secret of the return of the priceless El Greco collection as he inspected the patterns on the vases.

'What's your name?' enquired the General.

'You can call me Kun.'

The General was not sure whether this was the Chinaman's real name, but that was of far less concern to him right now than the news from his old and devoted servant. 'I'm glad to be receiving you here as a guest at my home. To what do I owe the pleasure?'

Fitz put the notebook down on the torpedo-shaped table. 'The Meander pattern has just lit up. Kun knows more about it. He has the same notebook and would like to speak to you further, General.'

The General switched to Cantonese. 'Tell me about the notebook, Kun. It's a new invention rather than an antique.'

'I was acting in accordance with Lu's wishes.'

'Lu Salome. Let's talk about her, then, if it's so important. What relationship does she have with you?'

'I am her only relative and family confidante.'

'Her last will and testament brings to light part of the history of the case of Miller's daughter.'

'Lu had a tattoo – an ouroboros.'

Kun took out a notebook that looked the same as the one on the table and held it out to the General.

'This device was confiscated from Hoffman. He caused interference again and died. Shredingers Cat -de-energized. And this is the merit of this young man,' said General.

'Lu turned out to be a talented progammer. Dresses and Jackets are her music and mathematics.' Fits meanwhile was examining the Chinese vase in the Secret Room. 'And help Sara Miller got rid of migraines.'

'What is Simon opinion on the score, Fitz?'

'The report about the increased temperature in the lake and the biosphere on the day Lu died due to the interference has been confirmed.' Fitz turned to face then. 'The largest glacier in the Alps is nearby. It was only by a miracle that this did not lead to catastrophic consequences. We can conclude the real threat lies not in the devices but in the synchroniser.

'The Hoffman container was not empty,' continued Kun. 'It was filled with a bunch of inexpensive trinkets with the addition of one metal.'

'A bonus in a game called "Dresses". That's why Giovanni *was arrested in the Chueca. He is confessing that he was looking for the Casket of Mazarin.* And no doubt why he found a way to the Reverend's heart so easily.'

'To the Casket of Mazarin, to be exact. There were no stones from the treasury of Mazarin – cheap earrings, but there were several Cufflinks with gemstones. And drawings of all the water resources were found at Hoffman's residence,' Kun reported as the General closed the notebook. 'In addition, Kun ready to present evidence that Hoffman was involved in the death of Miller's daughter.'

'The devices are yours, Kun.' The General handed him the notepad with the Meander, and the Chinaman nodded in gratitude.

'I will pass the information onto your man as soon as there is any news. You know, the auctioneers at Christie's think that the portrait concealed beneath Gainsborough's painting isn't his mother at all but his lover.'

'The main thing, I would suggest, is that the canvas is not a fake, wouldn't you say? The painting's value will go up a hundredfold if anything. An art connoisseur like you ought to attend such an auction.'

'It's time I was going – I don't want to miss it,' Kun replied, reverting to English.

One of the visitors had left the Secret Room.

'Could I ask you to talk in person?' Fitz took out the Montblanc fountain pen.

'You have a pen that is similar to a device for sending radio-wave signals. It appears to have saved your life.'

'My mother is TRANSITION KEEPER. I would like to see her.'

'It does not take a lot of time. I will give you the coordinates, Fitz.'

General courteously let Fitz to the door, Richard appeared from behind the ebony door, looking concerned. 'I haven't found any copies of Fitz,' he revealed.

The General became lost in thought, *Then where can the copies of the daughter have come from?*

'It's not out of the question that those of Alice were Taylor's handiwork. It could be his way of trying to protect her from danger,' Richard replied in answer to a question the General had not asked.

'Richard, tell Taylor he can do whatever he considers necessary,' the General instructed, who was sure that the trust demonstrated by his choice of words would delight him.

The British Museum

Richard and Taylor were on the top floor of the castle, drinking their evening tea. Taylor gazed into his face, in whose eyes one used to be able to read the clouds.

'A magical place,' enthused Taylor. 'It's where the venerable Margaret Evans was born.'

'So, the genuine Schrödinger cat is in a mousetrap?' Richard pressed.

'So, the Reverend lost both of them. Fitz is definitely not his son. That's why his fate so often smiles on him.'

'Is it difficult to keep other people's secrets, Richard?'

'No harder than your own, Taylor. How is your acquaintance, Simon?'

'Same as ever. He is looking for the twelfth rock in the garden at Ryōan-ji, but he has no desire to know where Margaret is—if indeed she is still alive. For Simon, the venerable Miss Evans was always the ideal.'

'The TRANSITION KEEPER programme became his life's passion – Simon. Today is my first day without the General. He managed to restore the operations carried out on Hoffman's computer, which he left behind amid the chaos in the restaurant beside the Douro. I know that Hoffman was looking for this man.'

Taylor glanced at the image.

'I knew Taylor. He was an honourable man from the north of the county of Cornwall,' Richard continued. 'Did you change your name before he ordered you to take care of Margaret?'

'I took Taylor's name here, which was also where his life ended.'

'Then you decided to help her flee from the house in Austria?'

'She loved that house but was never happy in it. Margaret had worked out what the General was plotting and was the first to smile at me.'

'Margaret made an impression on everyone ... no drones fly over the Alps when the weather is foggy. I only communicated with the TRANSITION KEEPER programme remotely,' Richard explained.

'For years she kept silent, but during the Transition in Portugal, she decided to ask some children the way to the temple where the Sacred Heart of Jesus Sanctuary was located. The people who knew of the programme's existence may have been able to determine her location.'

'What did the children say?' Richard asked.

'All three pointed in a different direction to the top of the Holy Mount.

'I am touched by the trust you are placing in me, Richard.'

'Simon received a message in "exceptional circumstances. I shall leave Harris's chess set, Taylor. New Babylon has renewed its work. Alice and Fitz will have access to it after the Transition is completed.'

Richard made out the code through the General's eyes. 'What is the threat?'

'A new Dictator would come to power. The war is already here.'

The Castle, Britain

The road map took Fitz from England to an estate, the former owner of which lived a short distance away. Following a road accident, he had completely turned his back on his various forms of social and religious charitable work and sold the land to a US corporation, while his garage containing his classic cars had been turned into a public museum. The woman who lived with him, a distant relative, rarely left the estate, and few people knew her; they used to say that she was the spitting image of the old lady who used to live in the castle. Fitz's search in this quiet England backwater was to be unsuccessful. To live all alone among such luxury. *This is the story of a man who has suffered serious trauma*, he thought, gazing at the enormous trees that neatly lined the driveway leading to the wooden door of the castle. Towards dusk. The lights were on in the castle and the door was hospitably open.

When he arrived, the door opened, and he walked into the empty castle unimpeded; it still seemed to give him a warm welcome. Its interior was richly decorated and yet at the same time uncomplicated. The walls were hung with freshly-bought paintings, abstracts and watercolours, that were clearly composed by two artists who painted in different styles. The library differed from the other rooms, for it was designed entirely in the Victorian style. As he gazed at them, he failed to notice that an unknown man was observing him.

Fitz could only make out a silhouette.

'These are my canvas. Do you like them?' the stranger enquired.

'Forgive me—art is not my strong point,' Fitz replied, confused. Taylor took a good look at Fitz and changed the settings.

'There's no need to apologise, Fitz. I planned your visit. I've been waiting for you.'

Fitz sensed the vibrations of the conversation with the whale, as he had on his graduation night when he had started to understand the unknown language of the seas and breathed in a forgotten scent.

Fitz saw the disguise change to another man wearing a neckerchief. He recognised the figure as his mother.

'We were happy together for a long time… but I'm not sure I'll be able to withstand all of my vital balances for long. Alice found some documents that confirmed that, under a mutual agreement, the estate next door belongs not to the corporation but to you and Alice. And the big black yacht *the Princess* is mine too.'

Fitz could see the hurt in his eyes. Tears started in Fitz's eyes. The long-forgotten smell of the sea and the oceans came back to him too. It was as if he had known the man with the handkerchief around his neck for a long time. 'Was he a racing driver, that man?'

'Constant pain syndrome, after the accident. I learned to reduce my threshold. After the Transition, the syndrome came back. After I have completed my task, the responsibility for the world remains with you.' She handed him the chip. 'Here are the monologues of the New Babylon, I have converted all audio and video information into text.'

'Your sister is in the garden, Fitz. Hers is the sky; yours, the earth. I shall be with you in spirit, my son. At all times, and whatever may happen.'

Fitz ran out of the room. The path led him to a secret garden where a light was burning. Three identical little girls were in the stone garden, two of whom immediately turned away. Behind them stood the Chinese Anthony.

'Hi, Fitz. Are you crying?' Alice asked.

The other Alice shook her head. 'My brother never cries.'

Meanwhile, the third Alice continued to carefully examine the flowerbeds with their arrays of flowers. Fitz caught sight of the notebook in her hand with the flickering Meander pattern. She had finished putting data into it.

'We meet at last!' said the first Alice. 'The world is ours.'

'But Alice – who are those two? Are they just like you?' Fitz asked, glancing to either side. Just like the real Alice, they were studying the hydroponics devices in the flowerbeds.

'They're my two copies. A new kind of genetic virus that quickly reproduces and spreads in conditions of fluctuating heat could present an unprecedented threat.'

'The temperature of the Earth is rising. We must now study the principle of vital functions for plant cultures,' said the second copy. In a couple of hours, we achieved more than Wisley Garden managed in years, another copy concluded.

The two copies smiled their identical smiles at him before his sister gave up her study of the new devices and looked at him more attentively. Fitz took the notebook from her.

'I've seen something like this twice before,' he recalled. As he pressed on the Meander, the notebook rapidly filled up with a list of first names and surnames in a variety of languages—he could not tear his gaze away from the pages of the notebook. He received a message from Kun on his phone stating that the two other devices had been synchronised.

'Don't forget about the pain, Fitz,' he heard his mother's voice whisper. Alice pressed the button and shot her brother a glance packed with gigabytes of information.

'When her voice leads us into an attack on the earth and in the sky, do not be afraid, sister. We Never Died.'

'The Meander blinked. You will lead the great battle on earth from the sky,' the Chinese Anthony said. At that moment, a bird fluttered out of the house and soared into the air. The copies of Alice vanished and turned into clouds.

Iridescent butterflies and birds soared upwards from the fields in little cyclones. The horizon at the end of the meadows was filled with colours. The wind had picked up some poplar catkins. As they fell to the ground, the butterflies and birds hid in the fields once more, and the clouds turned into a pod of whales. Alice put her strong palm into Fitz's hand as 'Für Elise' was heard playing in the sky. He had had an epiphany: Beethoven had not been deaf after all.

Richard was climbing up to the top floor via the narrow staircase. He opened the door. Immediately sensing Margaret's presence, however, he stopped himself from turning on the light.

'My dear, make me wait till the end of my days to see you again?'

'I will wait with you until dawn, Richard.'

We have finally reached the place.

Richard was about to turn on the light inside the cathedral but, sensing Margaret's presence, he stopped himself from doing so the sky and stars began to become visible through the cupolas.

He buried his face in Margaret's hair and whispered his final words:

'The sun and the stars were rebelling

O'er snow and light, I trod
And you alone in sorrow are dwelling
And you alone are my God.'

When the dawn came, their gentle breathing stopped. As they passed away. 'I'm coming to you, Margaret' – but Dark Domes did not hear the light tread of his son heading upstairs.

The General set off towards Maison Assouline, where Simon had been waiting for him. He handed the General a box containing a woman's revolver, inscribed with the words: 'This is the property of M.E.' In his fit of passion, your cousin left this behind on the Red Sea coast. 'New Babylon has successfully completed its mission. And send me a message. This is all that's left of Transition Kepper after integration, General. Pure sheet of paper?

'Not at all, the Transition time allows for unification with the entire network during the transition. They are all waiting for the signal,' said the General.

The black watch on his wrist signalled that they were entering the final minutes of the transition.

The Reverend stopped hiccupping as the General disappeared. The light fell through the door that stood ajar, and a piece of fluff floated in on the draught from his departure, slowly wending its way through the empty space until the door of the Secret Room closed automatically.